W9-BYJ-205

THE
BROCCOLI
TAPES

THE BROCCOLI TAPES

Jan Slepian

AN
APPLE
PAPERBACK

SCHOLASTIC INC.
New York Toronto London Auckland Sydney

No part of this publication may be reproduced in whole or in part, or stored in a retrieval system, or transmitted in any form or by any means, electronic, mechanical, photocopying, recording, or otherwise, without written permission of the publisher. For information regarding permission write to Philomel Books, a Division of the Putnam & Grosset Group, 200 Madison Avenue, New York, NY 10016.

ISBN 0-590-29321-4 (meets NASTA specifications)

Text copyright © 1988 by Jan Slepian. All rights reserved. Published by Scholastic Inc., 730 Broadway, New York, NY 10003, by arrangement with Philomel Books, a Division of the Putnam & Grosset Group. APPLE PAPER-BACKS is a registered trademark of Scholastic Inc.

2 3 4 5 6 7 8 9 10   40   00 99 98 97 96 95 94

Printed in the U.S.A.

First Scholastic printing, August 1990

For Richy, Cynthia, Danny and Clifford,
who were there.

THE
BROCCOLI
TAPES

TAPE 1

Click. Testing. One, two, three, four. Testing. Is this tape recorder working? This is Sara Davidson reporting from the moon. Calling Miss Hasselbauer and all the kids in sixth grade, Room 206, Baldwin School, Boston, Massachusetts, U.S.A., Planet Earth. Is anybody out there? It doesn't feel like it from here. *Click.*

Click. Hi, everybody. Here's my first tape. I tried lots of times, Miss Hasselbauer, but I couldn't get started. I'm so far away and there's so much to tell. I decided the best thing is to jump right in.

Today is Saturday, so I could sleep late, but like always the birds woke me up. It was just getting light, and I can hear them right outside my room. They go like this, coo-coo-coo, like they are gargling. The first week I thought they were in the room with me, that's how close they are. Now I know the fat little gray things are out in the garden behind the screen wall. I can't see them because of the blanket hanging there, but I can hear them.

I couldn't go back to sleep, so I went to wake up my brother Sam. He started middle school here, so I hardly see him anymore.

He's a slow waker. Sometimes he has to be dragged out of bed and stood up on his feet while he's still asleep, no kidding. My mother has to tell him left foot, right foot, just to get him going. This morning I pushed him hard. He pulled the sheet over his head and I pulled it off.

"Wake up," I said, "There's a tidal wave coming, and it's going to cover the whole island. We're lost."

He opened one eye and said, "Okay," and went back to sleep again.

I noticed a calendar on the wall above his head. It had all the days we've been here crossed out, three weeks of crosses. I didn't know he was keeping track.

I said in his ear, "Let's cross off another day," and that did it. He really woke up then. He kneeled on the bed and crossed out today, January 28. Then he lifted up the pages to May one by one. That's how many uncrossed days there are left to go. I wish they were all crossed off right now.

Sam said to get dressed, we're going someplace, he had something to show me.

I was surprised. Usually he never wants me along. "What something?" I asked. But he wouldn't say.

Everybody was still asleep, so we left a note on the kitchen table.

When we stepped outside, the sky was pinking up. There's probably still snow on the ground in Boston. You guys still have your boots on, and I'm walking around barefooted. Here there are palm trees and the air smells like flowers. From our front door I can see a green mountain with houses and streets going up the sides. Our house is higher than the ones across the way, and over the rooftops I can see the ocean spread to nowhere. The hedge in front of our house has red flowers on it big as plates. I picked one and stuck it behind my ear just like in the magazine you showed us, Miss Hasselbauer. Hawaii is really beautiful, if you don't count all the buildings.

Before we left home my father showed us on a map where he had rented a house for us. He told us, "It's on a narrow strip of land that juts out into the ocean. If you think of it as a finger, we are almost at the nail."

So we walked along, headed for the nail, and I knew that at the end of it was nothing but ocean. I also knew we couldn't get there, because a few houses down there's a chain across the road. Mom told me that it was there to keep people out, that beyond the chain was private property and not to go there.

Sam ducked under it and said, "Come on."

I was a little nervous about this. "We can be put in jail for this."

He said, "Not me. I'll tell them it was your idea." He flashed his braces at me, so I knew he was kidding. Sometimes with him I can't tell.

Pretty soon we were at the tip of the finger, and what Sam wanted to show me stopped my breath.

There was this whole field full of crazy rocks, big black ones that tumbled every which way down to the ocean. Nothing else. Only sky and ocean and those weird, funny-shaped rocks. It was like we had come to the end of the world. Or more like the beginning of it. In that place I could imagine dinosaurs.

"What are these things?" I asked Sam. Up close they were all rough and had holes in them like Swiss cheese.

Sam told me they were lava rocks. He said, "This whole island is made of lava, and these got left over. They've been here forever." He stroked one of them without looking, like he was blind and was knowing it by touch. Then he bent down and licked it!

"What are you doing?" I couldn't imagine.

"I wanted to know what old tastes like," he said. My brother Sam is a very odd person. He was in your class once, Miss Hasselbauer, so you must know what I mean.

He started jumping from one rock to another, heading for the ocean. There's a big pile of these rocks where the lava field ended down by the water, like a long wall to keep the ocean out. I could see the spray from the waves shooting up from the other side. I followed Sam.

The closer I got to where the waves crashed, the more misty it got, like walking into the softest shower. I stopped and spread my arms and turned around in it, wanting to fly.

I looked around for Sam to tell him to come under the shower with me. I couldn't see him anywhere. The lava field was so empty, I felt like I was the only person in the whole world. Then I saw his head pop up from the middle of the field and disappear and then pop up again. He was looking for something.

When I caught up with him, he put his finger to his lips. "Shhh," he said. "Listen. Don't you hear something?"

I did. But because of the noise of the waves, I couldn't make out what it was.

We followed the sound closer to the ocean. It grew louder, and now I could make out an awful howl. Like something in pain.

I knew what it was. "An animal!" I said.

"A cat," said Sam.

He was right. It was caught between two rocks, just the leg. The rocks must have moved a little and trapped him. We figured out that maybe the heavy pounding of the waves shifted them just enough to do it. Anyway, it was terrible. I never saw a trapped animal in person before. He was screeching and pulling and snapping at his leg. I had read about a trapped animal sometimes gnawing its own leg off to free itself, and now I could believe it.

Sam was studying what to do, but I couldn't wait. I began pulling at one of the rocks that held him and yelled for Sam to help. He pushed and I pulled, and finally, finally, when we were just about to give up, we moved it and the cat yanked his leg free.

It lay on the ground like it was dead, only its sides were pumping. We were really able to look at it then. It was the worst-looking cat I ever saw. It was scarred up and bald in spots. You could see patches of naked gray skin. One ear was torn. The fur was no color, a kind of rusty old black, like the rocks. And of course, his poor bloody leg.

We didn't know what to do next. We just couldn't leave it there to die.

Sam said, "Let's get it some food."

Its ribs were sticking out. He was starving. I so

wanted to show him that we were friends. What popped into my head was that story about a mouse taking a thorn out of a lion's paw and the lion said only call on him, he would do the mouse a favor someday. I wanted the cat to know who saved him.

I reached out to pet him, and if the cat knew we saved his life, he didn't think it was a favor. As soon as my hand came near he turned on me, his teeth showing, ready to bite.

Sam said to leave him alone. He was going to run home and get some food and I should stay with the cat.

So I was sitting on that rock, wishing that Sam would hurry up. The cat was still there, but it's a lonesome place to be. Just these old, old rocks and all that ocean and sky. Birds were swooping out of the sky and landing on the wall. I could hear them peeping to one another like deserted babies. It all made me feel shivery, even though it was as warm as summer.

I heard someone say, "How come you killed that cat?" *Click.*

Click. Sorry about that. It's late, and I'm still not used to the night noises here. See, right outside my room here is the garden. I'm always hearing funny noises out there. Nothing really. Just my imagination.

So I was telling you, someone said, "How come you killed that cat?" and behind me was this boy. He was throwing a stone up and catching it, and looking at me with his squinty black eyes. He's about Sam's age, but a shrimp. I'm even taller than he is. He looked like a lot of kids I see around, straight black hair, the kind that fits like a bathing cap, and shiny brown skin. Only, this kid was dirty. His tank top and cutoffs looked like they'd never been washed even once.

I was so mad. I said, "He's not dead! We saved his life. You weren't even here."

What he did was throw that stone. He was aiming at the birds on the wall.

"You're the one who wants to hurt something around here," I told him.

"Wouldn't mind," he said. He wasn't kidding, and that's when I began to get scared. I was alone, see? And he had plenty of muscles and he wasn't a bit friendly. In fact, he was the worst person I ever met. I began looking around for a stick or a stone, just in case. I didn't want him to see what I was doing, but he saw, all right.

He saw and he didn't pay any attention. He said, "What do you think you are going to do with that cat?"

I haven't said yet that he was hard to understand. He spoke in a kind of singsong like a lot of kids here, what they call pidgin. I was getting on to it. I can't imitate him, Miss Hasselbauer. I know I'm to report what people say, but I'm just telling it straight.

I said, "Feed it. I don't know, maybe take it home." I knew I couldn't do that. My father is allergic, and we were never allowed to have pets.

"Take it home." He acted like I had said something funny. "Whaddaya, crazy? Don't they teach you nothing where you come from? You won't tame that thing in a million years. It's wild. It'll snap your

15

head off soon as look at you. Hey, haole, where you from?"

I'm used to being called haole from school here. It means stranger, and that's how it makes you feel. "Boston," I told him. "My father is teaching biology here for a while, so we all had to come. You from around here?"

He looked all around that beautiful place, up at the sky and around the lava field and then back at me. He spit on his rock like he was disgusted. "Yeah," he said, "In some dump across the parkway. What's it to you?"

"What are you so mad at?" I said. "I didn't do anything to you."

Just then I saw Sam jumping rocks, coming toward us. He had his hands full of food. For once I was glad to see him. "There's my brother," I said, standing up and waving.

Sam was as out of breath as if he had run the marathon. He's really in bad shape. That's because he hates exercise. He was a couple of rocks away when he began calling out what he was carrying, "Bread, milk, tuna fish," like he was reading off a menu.

I looked down, and the cat wasn't there anymore. I felt terrible. It must have gotten away while I was talking to that boy. Then, when I wanted to ask him if he saw the cat get away, the boy was gone also. I could see the back of him already far away, leaping the rocks like somebody was chasing him.

Sam saw him and asked, "Who's that?"

I didn't want to talk about him. I just pointed to the empty space where the cat was supposed to be.

I was so disappointed. Sam was okay about it. He didn't yell. We decided to leave the food there anyway, just in case. We even left the bowl he brought for the milk.

On the way home, Sam said, "There's one good thing. It means he can walk. It means maybe we'll see him again."

"Who?" I asked.

"The cat, of course! Who do you think I meant?"

So then I told Sam all about the awful boy.

I have to go now, and I hardly got started. It's been some day.

I hope this is what you want for the Oral History project, Miss Hasselbauer. It got easier as I went along. *Click.*

Click. Hi to nobody. Just to me. I know how to erase whatever I want to on this tape. So this part I will.

Miss Hasselbauer's my princess! When I told her that my family was going to Hawaii for five whole months, she thought I was crying because of leaving my friends. Well, I was, but also because of having to leave her. That's why I was so glad when she said I could still be part of the Oral History project for social studies. It means she's still my teacher. She knew I felt bad about everybody in class making tapes about their family and all. Everybody but me. She said I could still do it, that all I have to do is to be a good reporter and remember what people say. She would play the tapes back in class, and that way we would keep in touch.

The thing is, I couldn't get started. It was so aggravating, because I'm such a talker. But every time I thought of the whole sixth grade listening to me, I got self-conscious. Also, there's too much to tell. It's different when you live in a place and are not just there for a visit.

I told this to Grandma. She's having a terrible vacation here. She doesn't feel well and just sits on the recliner in our living room most of the day. She keeps looking out at the ocean. She doesn't stop looking at the view even when we're talking, like she's hanging on to it. That's not like Grandma. She's always so up and doing.

First Grandma said to me, "Five months isn't living here, it's just an eyeblink." Maybe to her, but not to me. Then, when I told her about my trouble with taping, she said, "You, self-conscious, Sara? I'm surprised."

I hate it when somebody close shows they don't know me. Lots of times I don't show the way I really feel. She should know that. She isn't concentrating on me the way she usually does.

But she did help me about these tapes.

She asked me if I was making the tapes for that teacher I'm so crazy about. When I told her that I was, she said, "So why don't you just talk to her. Forget about the class. Put her in front of your mind and say what you want to her. Like she's in the room with you."

So that's how I finally got started today. But I don't like to tell even Miss Hasselbauer how it really is. It makes me shiver if I think people feel sorry for me. If I talked about how lonesome I am and how bad things are for me here, she would. The whole class would.

I tried talking to Mom about how it is for me here. I didn't even get halfway started when she pressed her hand to her eyes the way she does when she's trying hard to be patient.

She said to me, "Look, Sara, I can't deal with this right now. Go talk to your father. That's a good girl." I know it's because she's worried about Grandma, but even so. Mom always used to know when I needed her. And I can't tell Daddy either, because he doesn't like to hear troubles. He wants us only to have a good time, because he brought us here, he's responsible.

Mainly, it's school. I don't know what the rules are or how to be. Yesterday was so awful. We're doing the Lewis and Clark Expedition in social studies. I know all that from last year. So Mrs. Chun was asking questions about it, and I was the only one answering. I was raising my hand, and I knew the answers, and I thought, hey good, finally they'll know I'm alive.

Well, in the cafeteria not even Doris Nakamura would speak to me, and she's the only one even halfway friendly so far. I don't know what I did that was so bad. Well, I guess I do know, but that's what we do at home. Raise our hands and speak up. Here they think it's show-offy.

I thought it would help if I talked about it—even to a machine. It doesn't. What I think is that I'm going to die of lonesomeness here. *Click.*

Click. Hi, everybody, I'm back. It's Sunday morning, and I have lots to tell you.

I think I left off when we were going home yesterday morning after leaving the food for the cat we rescued. Well, know what? We got into trouble over that bowl Sam took from the kitchen for the cat's milk. We were going to go back for it later, but Mom found out first.

We didn't say anything about the cat when we got home. We knew better. Daddy was messing around in the kitchen making pancakes. That's his specialty on Saturday mornings. He was singing. A very good sign. He has a terrible voice, but I love it when he sings.

When we walked in, he said, "Just in time. Big treat this morning. I put macadamia nuts in the batter, and I'm about to start cooking. Go call the ladies. Where have you two been? I was hoping you ran away." People think my father is always so serious, maybe because he looks like one of those absentminded professor types. But that's because they don't know him. He can be crazy, and also he teases a lot.

Sam told him we were out for a walk like the note said. He told him about the lava field at the end of the road, but he didn't mention the cat. I left them talking away about geology and went to find my grandmother. She was already sitting in her chair in front of the big window.

She didn't hear me come in, and there was something about her that stopped me. It made me think of what my mom said when we first met my grandmother at the airport. Mom said to my father, "Dear God, what's the matter with her?"

I always like the way my grandma looks, because she doesn't wear too much makeup and her hair is always fixed. She's fat, but her dresses are pretty. She lives all alone in a tiny apartment in New York City and sells baby clothes in a department store. That's why she always looks good. She once told me she has to keep up appearances because she serves the public. Mom says she's had a hard life bringing up two children by herself and having to work, too. I never even knew my grandfather.

So when we met her at the airport, I didn't think anything was the matter. I didn't know what my mother meant. Grandma looked the same to me, only very white. But lots of tourists look like that when they get off the plane. Especially if they come from someplace cold in the winter. So she was pale and her clothes didn't fit anymore. I could see that. I just thought she was on a diet. She was always saying she didn't understand why she was fat when she didn't eat that much. Mom would laugh at her and tell her about the cream she puts in her coffee and the Danish she has for breakfast.

I remember how glad she was to see us. She and Mom just held on and on. Then we hung the leis around her neck. That's the custom here when a visitor comes. They get flowers and a kiss. Isn't that a beautiful custom, Miss Hasselbauer? I'm going to keep doing that wherever I am, not just here.

My grandmother's back hurts and she doesn't feel like eating. It's spoiling her vacation. Mom says unless she improves in a few days she'll take her to a doctor. I hate the way my mother holds up a spoon to her, coaxing her to eat like she was a baby. My grandma isn't a baby.

I was thinking of all this when I was watching her in

the recliner chair. What she was doing was bending over, swaying back and forth holding on to herself. Her face was white, but white all the way through, not just tourist pale. I could really see that now. I can't explain how she was. Like she was listening to something deep in her own self. There was something so different about her that I ran and knelt in front of her and put my arms around her waist and hung on.

She lifted my chin and tried to smile and said, "What's this? What's this so early in the morning? Did you have a bad dream?"

I said, "How do you feel today, Grandma?" as if I couldn't see with my own eyes.

"I'm fine, my darling. Just a little indisposed. It'll pass."

"Then come have breakfast. Daddy says the pancakes are ready."

"You know, I think I'll skip it this morning. Do me good. Look out there. See how that ocean changes all the time? It moves and moves and goes on forever. Isn't that a miracle? Look at those clouds. Everything I see out there is a miracle." You would think she never saw water or sky before.

She made me go to breakfast, and Mom took her in some soda water, which is all she lives on these days. We talked about Grandma at the table. Mom says she made a doctor's appointment on Wednesday. I forgot all about the cat.

Then, after, I was in here in my room reading *The Prince and the Pauper*, which I really love, my mother came in, all puzzled. She doesn't walk, she bounces, and already I'm almost as tall as she is. She was about to say something when she stopped and pointed to the pink blanket on the wall. She said, "Can't we take that down yet?"

I have to explain something. When we first came here, it was late and dark outside. We were all walking around this house seeing what we were going to be living in for months. When we came to this room, my mother said, "How perfect, Sara. This will be your room. Don't you love it? You're practically outdoors."

That was the trouble. There's this one whole wall with just a screen on it. A bed was in front of it, my bed it was going to be. The only thing between me and the black outside was that screened wall. I'm not usually afraid of the dark, but I was in a strange place. I could hear the wind rubbing the leaves in the garden, and they sounded like fingers. The wall looked like a big black hole ready to swallow me. It was like when I was a little kid and my open closet door had monsters in it.

My father took one look at me and said right away, "I'll fix that."

He found a blanket from someplace and tacked it over the screen, so now I have a pink wall. No, I'm not ready to take it down yet. I told that to my mother.

She didn't argue; she had come in for something else. She said, "There's a bowl missing from the kitchen, Sara. A small china bowl. Do you know anything about this?"

I didn't have to say anything. My face always gives me away when I'm caught. It gets so hot and so red that Sam once told me you could read by it. My mom saw right away that I knew what she was talking about.

So I told her about rescuing the cat and what the bowl was for. What she did was call my father in and say, "Listen to this." Then he called Sam in. Four of us in my tiny room.

I saw an old Marx Brothers movie once on TV where lots of people crowded into a stateroom on a ship. Did any of you ever see it? They were piled one on top of another, and more kept coming in. That's not exactly what was going on, but it was close enough to remind me. I giggled when I thought of it. My father wanted to know what was so funny.

He said, "You think contact with a wild and possibly diseased animal is a joke?" He was really angry, or more like scared for us, I don't know.

I was on my bed, and the three of them had just enough room to stand up. No place to sit. If one more person came in, somebody would have to stand on the bed. I told him what I was thinking of, and since he loves the Marx Brothers he laughed too, and so did Mom. Thank you, Marx Brothers.

My father gave us this big talk about abandoned animals and what happens to them. He said, "We are on a tiny dot in the middle of the Pacific, and it isn't easy to take a pet back to the mainland. Many people don't want the trouble and expense, so they turn them loose. It's cruel, but that's what they do. And then what happens? That animal turns wild. A wild cat can be dangerous. You understand what I'm saying?"

Mom interrupted, because she wanted Dad to get to the point. "That cat could have rabies for all we know. Never touch it! Promise me."

I noticed Sam was nodding his head up and down like he agreed completely, the rat.

I could hardly speak. I said, "First you say it's cruel to leave them, and now you want us to. Our cat isn't sick, it's just hungry. Don't you have any pity?"

Mom said, "Keep your voice down. I don't want your grandma to hear this. She doesn't need to be upset."

Dad said, "You're the heartless one, Sara. If you keep on feeding this cat, it will become dependent on you for its food. It will lose the ability to fend for itself. You think that's a favor? You know, of course, you will have to leave it here when we go home."

It wasn't a question. I knew that for sure. But all I could see in my mind was that poor homeless cat. Probably dying to have someone pet him. Dependent on us, my father had said. That sounded pretty good to me.

Dad said, "Do you understand what I'm saying, Sam?"

Sam the traitor said, "Sure. I'll go get the bowl."

"Me too," I said.

"Be careful," Mom called after us.

When we got outside, Sam turned on me like I had done something terrible. He was squeaking angry. Usually you can never tell what Sam is feeling. If he has any feelings at all, he keeps them to himself.

"What did you tell them for! You queered the whole thing." His voice is changing, and it shot way up.

"That's not fair! You're the one. 'Sure, Dad, I understand, Dad. No more cat.' I heard you."

Well, he told me he was just putting on an act for our parents and I was dumb not to know it. I bet if you had been there Miss Hasselbauer, you would have been fooled too.

Anyway we were hurrying along the road arguing

like this. When we got to the lava field, he said, "Listen, we don't even know if the cat is there anymore. But if he is, we're going to take care of him. We'll have to go underground with this thing, understand? No more talking. They aren't going to change their minds, so that's that. This cat is a secret. He's ours. They don't have to know a thing about it. He has nobody, no home, nothing. He needs us."

Sam was all worked up. He has this white skin that blondies have sometimes, and he gets all red and splotchy when he's upset. He looked like he had a rash like poison ivy.

It was almost funny. Here we were, getting all excited over a cat that wasn't there. But what Sam said about it having nobody and being homeless was true. The cat's like us. We don't have any friends, and we're homeless too. We have a lot in common.

Nobody was at the lava field. I made sure the angry boy wasn't around. I sure didn't want to bump into him again.

We started jumping the rocks, but we couldn't figure out where we left the food. They all look pretty much the same. I mean, we didn't know which one was the rescue rock.

Sam was talking to himself. "What a dumb thing. I should have marked it. I could have tied my shoelace to it, or piled some pebbles. I could have left my shirt. I should have left the food on top."

He went on and on, and I left him to explore by myself. I was the one to find the rock.

"Over here!" I yelled.

We looked down at the empty bowl. The can of tuna

26

fish was also empty. Not even a crumb of bread was left.

It was some feeling.

Then, just like Daddy, Sam got logical on me. "How do we know it was our cat that ate it? Maybe there are lots of stray cats here. How do we know that?"

I didn't want to hear that. I told him, "It was, it was our cat. I know it." To tell the truth, it was more wanting and hoping than knowing.

And then—magic. As if he heard me, or like in a fairy tale you get your wish, the cat was suddenly there. We didn't see him come. Just all of a sudden he was on the rock opposite, like he was dropped from the sky.

Miss Hasselbauer, remember when we were talking about clichés in class, and you said to try not to use tired old sayings in composition? I think one of them was "an answer to a prayer." I have to tell you that's exactly what it felt like. That, and another one on the list: "a sight for sore eyes." Exactly. I'm not using them, I'm just telling how they fit.

Our cat let us watch him for a long while. It was him all right, because we could see the torn ear and the bald spots and the raw place on his leg where the rock had grabbed him. He's a mess. But I don't care, that doesn't matter.

He stood like a statue, with one paw lifted, looking off someplace else, not at us. It was like he was saying, "Go ahead, admire me, ain't I beautiful?" He didn't move, but he made you know he was smelling and hearing and seeing—everything. His black head was up, and then he slowly turned it to us. Yellow eyes that looked like they knew every secret in the world. Everything about him fit the lava field, like he was one of the old rocks turned into a cat. I've seen cats before, and believe me, he's special. Take my word for it, he has a great personality.

I held my hand out to him, puss, puss, puss. If my mother had seen that, she would have died. But she needn't have worried, he didn't take any notice of me at all. He held his pose for maybe a few seconds more and then he sprang away. He disappeared in the rocks like we had dreamt him up.

Sam and I didn't say a word after. We picked up the empty can of tuna fish and the bowl my mom was asking for and got ourselves back on the road.

Before we went into the house Sam grabbed my shoulder. He said, "We're going to feed that cat every day. So just remember, no talking."

I told him that he didn't have to remind me, I know how to keep a secret better than he does. But he didn't answer my question. I had asked him, "Without Mom and Dad knowing, where do we get the food?" He doesn't know the answer, and neither do I.

Sorry, I have to go now. Mom's calling me for breakfast. I still haven't finished yesterday. I haven't even gotten to the surprise yet. *Click.*

Click. I'm ready for bed, Miss Hasselbauer, and I have to keep my voice down, because my parents are in the room opposite. They know about these tapes, but it must sound pretty whacky in here, like I'm talking to myself. Also, I don't want them to hear anything about the cat.

I left off where we were returning the bowl. Mom took it from me like it was a dead rat. She held it by two fingers and her nose crinkled up like it smelled bad, which it didn't. She dumped it in the sink and ran hot water over it.

The only thing she said was, "You're not to take anything from this house again. Nothing here belongs to us."

Just hearing that, bang, I had a terrible fit of homesickness. That's exactly what's wrong here. Nothing is ours, nothing is home, and what came over me was wanting home so much. Do you know what I mean? I always thought I was big on adventure and going off by myself, like going around the world or living with wolves. Now I know different. Dreams like that are easy when you're home and everything is familiar.

Like a little kid, I ran to her. I said, "That's the worst thing I ever heard!"

She said, "Is it, now?" Her mouth was twitching, and she was ready to joke me out of it the way she used to. Then she changed. She looked past me through the door and into the living room where Grandma sat. She took a deep breath and then said on a sigh, "I hope you're right. I hope it will be the worst thing that ever happens to you."

Daddy came into the kitchen then. He opened one drawer after another, banging them shut like he was angry. He said, "Where are the tools in this house? Can you tell me where I can put my hands on a wrench, Delly? The bathroom faucet leaks."

Mom said, "The realtor left us a list of what's in the house. It's in that drawer there. I don't remember seeing any tools on the list, now that you mention it."

You would think she had just said there weren't any beds in the house, that's how amazed my father was. He said, "How can you run a house without tools?" like it was my mother's fault.

Mom just laughed at him. "It's not the end of the world," she said. "I have to go to the mall this afternoon anyway. I want to get Mother something more comfortable than those city clothes. A muumuu maybe. You want to come? You can buy a wrench. Take it home with you. You can always use a wrench, can't you?"

This was a joke, because my father is a big fix-it man and has more tools at home than a regular hardware store.

Daddy said, "Let's get going, then." He hates to go shopping, but mention buying tools and it's like he's going to a candy store.

Sam was there leaning against the sink. He was staring at the refrigerator. I could read his mind. He was thinking of all the food inside that we needed and couldn't take.

Mom asked us if we'd like to come along, or would we prefer to stay home and keep Grandma company? I thought it was a perfect chance to go back to the lava field. Maybe we'd see the cat again. But Sam looked me in the eye and told her sure we'd go, how about it Sara? I knew he had something in mind, Miss Hasselbauer, because with my brother sometimes his eyes say more than his mouth.

I found out in the car. He showed me three dollars and whispered that we could buy a bowl for our cat. Mom had to turn around and ask what all the excitement was about. I'm not used to keeping secrets from her, but I know now that it's a cinch.

We finally found a place to park at the mall, and we asked if we could go around by ourselves. Mom and Dad said okay, and that we were all to meet back at the mall escalator in an hour sharp.

I think Mom would have held on to us. She said, "Take care, you two. Stay together. And Sara, you keep an eye on the time." It's a family joke how Sam doesn't pay attention. His head is always someplace else. He's the absentminded professor in our family, not my father. Sometimes it's funny, and sometimes I could kick him for it.

My dad was impatient. "Come on, Delly. If they get lost, we can always make two more." He winked at us. I already said he liked to tease.

Usually I like to look at everything. I like to look in the store windows and smell the foods and see what people are wearing. When I shop with Mom, sometimes we sit on a bench and just watch the crowds go by, like watching a show. We make up stories about the people and have a good time. But this afternoon I was concentrating on just one thing. I wasn't interested in anything but finding the perfect bowl for our cat.

Sam must have been dreaming again, because he walked right by the pet store. I had to run and go get him.

In the window was the most wondrous thing. A white cat was curled up fast asleep on a throne. It looked like a snowball except for its long tail that hung over the side. My Aunt Carrie has an old white feather boa that I used for dress up. It looks just like that tail. The throne was gold and the cushion that the snowball cat was sleeping on was bright red. Never in my whole life have I seen anything like that for a pet. What a lucky cat.

There was a red carpet on the floor. It led to a doll castle as fancy as a picture in a fairy tale.

"Look at its beautiful house." I pointed it out to Sam. I so wanted to see inside. I could imagine a table set with a lace tablecloth and gold dishes. A bed with a silken canopy. A royal bathtub.

Sam said, "That's where they keep the kitty litter."

You can see why I hate my brother sometimes.

He tapped on the glass. "There it is!" he said. I hadn't noticed the bowl before. It was shiny white with the words "Princess Di" printed on it in red letters. A perfect bowl.

We went right into the store.

Inside, it was crowded and noisy. On one side, the puppies were yipping away in their tiny cages. On the other side, birds and guinea pigs were chirping and squealing. Down the center aisle were tanks and tanks of tropical fish. I didn't see any cats at all.

There were lots of little kids holding on to a grown-up's finger, walking by the cages like they were in a zoo.

I said to Sam, "What name should we put on the bowl?"

He said, "Let's find out how much it is first."

That's when I saw the angry boy from the lava field. He was kneeling in front of the guinea pig cages, changing the water or something, working there. That's the surprise I told you about. I couldn't believe it! Of all the places in the world, I wouldn't expect him to work in a pet store. He hates animals, I know it.

I yanked Sam's arm and told him who was there. He looked for himself and said, "Hey, I know him. I know that guy from school. He's in one of my classes. He's the one they call The Nut. That's his name, Eddie Nutt."

I said, "You know him, go ask about the bowl."

Sam said, "Not me. I saw him once punch a guy in the cafeteria over nothing, just for putting his tray down at the same table. Everybody keeps away from Eddie Nutt."

While we were talking, I didn't take my eyes away from Eddie for a minute. I saw a man walk over to him and tap him on the shoulder. I couldn't hear what they were saying, but both of them were angry.

He turned out to be Eddie's father. I know that because a lady nearby called out, "Oh Mr. Nutt, can I ask a favor?"

When he turned to her, right away I could see a resemblance. Eddie and his father didn't look at all alike, I don't mean that. His father had reddish hair and a big nose. Also, he was big and soft and hairy. He was all pink skin under the hair, while Eddie was as brown as the floor. Lots of people here are mixed-up races, so Eddie's mother must be something else. Maybe she's a true Hawaiian. If I ever speak to him again, which I doubt, I'm going to ask him.

Anyway, the alike part was more in the way they were when they were talking. Maybe it was the way their eyebrows went straight across. I don't know, but they had the same mean, unfriendly look.

The lady said, "My Wayne here has something on his mind. Go ahead, Wayne, ask Mr. Nutt."

Her little boy said something, and Mr. Nutt squatted down so he and the boy were more equal. I heard him say, "I didn't hear you. Come again?" Now he seemed like a nice man.

The boy said loud enough for me to hear, "Can I see your cat? Can I?"

Mr. Nutt said, "She's right there in the window. Sure you can see her."

Wayne's mother said, "He wants to pet her. I have to take him here to see Princess Di every time I go shopping. He pesters me about her all the time. Do you think this once he can see her up close? That's what you want to say to Mr. Nutt, isn't it, dearest?"

Eddie's father stood up and said, "I don't do this for everyone, but just this once, I'll get her for you, Wayne. She's a beauty all right." Anybody could see he was proud of that cat.

Eddie was busy with another cage, but I saw him looking at his father, who was being so nice. He was holding one of the guinea pigs in his hand and listening. Maybe he wasn't paying attention, because the pig got away. I actually saw it twist and shoot out of Eddie's hand.

Then, what a mess! It's like a blur now, because everything happened so fast. The pig was gone in a flash. A lady screamed, maybe because she felt it brush against her leg. Her child screamed because her mother did. Then it was like a scream plague had hit the store, most of it from kids having a wonderful time making noise, probably thinking it was a funny game. What I wish is that I had had this tape recorder with me so that you all could hear the commotion.

Eddie had gone after the guinea pig, and I didn't see him until he stood up with it squealing and twisting in his hands, holding it over his head to show his father that he had caught it. Mr. Nutt calmed everyone down, and it was over just like that. Maybe it all took only a couple of minutes, but Sam and I had a great time while it lasted.

Eddie put the guinea pig back in the cage right away, but he had to deal with his father. What I heard Mr. Nutt say to him was, "A careless no-good," also, "Your fault," and "More like her every day." Things like that. Right out loud. It was awful, not so much what he said but how he was with Eddie. I never saw a father who didn't like his own son before. His very own son. That would be so terrible.

I couldn't stand it, and Sam couldn't either. He did something I didn't know he had in him. He went right up to Mr. Nutt and said, "Excuse me. I have to tell you that what happened was my fault. I bumped into Eddie by mistake. I'm awfully sorry. That was how the guinea pig got away. Hey, Eddie, no hard feelings?"

Well, what could Mr. Nutt do then? He pulled at his nose and stared at Sam and then just dropped the whole thing. He said "Okay," and turned away. He went to the window to get Princess Di for Wayne, who was still waiting.

Wasn't that a great thing for Sam to do? You'd think

Eddie Nutt would be grateful, but he didn't even thank Sam. He didn't even look at Sam, as if he weren't there.

He said something to me, though. He said, "Well, look who's here. The cat killer."

I suppose I felt sorry for him, but disgusted, too. I said to my brother, "Let's get out of here." He didn't want to go before finding out about the bowl.

We left Eddie flat and went up to Mr. Nutt, much as I hated him. We had to wait while he held Princess Di out for the little boy to pet.

That is some beautiful cat. I thought of our poor starving one at the lava field. He had nothing, and this one had so much. It really isn't fair. You know how we talked in class about the poor homeless people living on the streets in Boston, Miss Hasselbauer? I said how unfair for some people to have so little and others so much, and how it makes my blood boil? Well, that's exactly how I feel about Princess Di and our cat.

Another thing that isn't fair is that Mr. Nutt was like the proudest person in the world showing off his pet. Those big, hairy hands of his stroked her so gently, and he actually stuck his nose in her fur and kissed her. You know what I think, Miss Hasselbauer? I think he likes the cat more than his own son.

Sam nudged me that it was my turn. I was very polite. I said, "Excuse me, could you tell us how much that bowl is in the window? Can we buy one?"

Mr. Nutt looked at me full then. And I saw . . . well, what jumped into my mind was what sad eyes, not mean but sad. I know how I imagine things. Mom is always telling me that I make a story out of nothing. But that's what I saw.

He said, "You can't buy that bowl, or any one like it in any store. I had it specially made. Sorry, little girl."

So that was that.

Sam says, no problem, we'll solve it. Tomorrow we are going to feed our cat again, but what, we don't know yet.

I just decided I'm going to send you this tape and start a new one. I'm so glad I finally got started. I don't want you to forget me. I haven't said anything about school yet, but there isn't that much to tell. It's different here, especially the people. I know how lucky you all think I am to be here, swimming and all. You won't believe me, but more than anything in the world I wish that I was back home again. *Click.*

Click. I'm starting on the second tape, and I never thought I could do even one. I sent you the first one last week, and maybe right now this minute you are listening to it. I see you all in class and Miss Hasselbauer is wearing her red jumper and there's my empty seat in the fourth row. Maybe somebody else is sitting in it, but I hope not.

I try not to think about home usually. It's too far away, and we still have four months to go. But when I'm sitting in class here and I know that no one cares if I'm here or not, I can't help it. I pretend it's you up there, Miss Hasselbauer, and that I'm where I belong. I dream all through class and no one knows. Recess, too. There's this bunch of girls who play double dutch on the driveway every day. I asked once if I could take an end, but Doris Nakamura, the one I thought I liked, said too many were playing already. I won't ask ever again. They could beg and I wouldn't. So what I do at recess is sit under a tree and dream away.

My father wrapped the cassette for me and said he would drop it off on his way to his office. But before he wrapped it, I had a scare. He asked if he could hear it. He knows I'm doing this Oral History project.

"Your mother and I would like to hear it" were his

exact words. I almost fainted. By now you know there were secrets. I mean, especially about the cat. I couldn't possibly.

It was almost funny how fast my mind raced around picking up one excuse after another in nothing flat. Then I found the magic words. "I'm sorry, it's private," I told him.

The word *private* is very big around my house ever since I opened a letter to my father from school here. This was when we first came and I thought it said something bad about me. It was nothing. They hadn't gotten my records yet, that's all. But when I saw the envelope and it was from my school, I tore it open. Miss Hasselbauer, I told you I was scared about going to a new school. Well, my father was angry about me opening his letter. He gave me this big lecture about privacy. So now he couldn't say a thing. I'll know next time to wrap the tape up myself.

We see our cat every day. After school I can't wait to go to the lava field. I drop my books off, pick up the bag of leftovers, and I run to him, so happy that he's there for me. Sam, too. I meet him there when he's through with school. For the first time we're like partners in something special. Mom and Dad are both so taken up with my grandmother that they hardly know we're around.

What we do is take the cat our leftovers. I mean, whatever we have left over from supper the night before, like bits of hamburger or bread, or like yesterday he ate up my baked potato. He doesn't mind. He's hungry enough to eat anything. He's not fussy like some cats. I bet Princess Di is fussy.

Mom hasn't noticed what we do with leftovers, except last night when we jumped up to clear. She probably thought we were so helpful about clearing because of Grandma. Actually, there are lots of reasons to want to get away from the table. Nobody talks much anymore. My stomach gets squeezed when Mom is so worried. Grandma's empty chair is the loudest thing there. She's in the hospital right now having tests to see what's wrong.

Anyway, last night when we got up to clear the table my mother caught hold of Sam's arm.

"Wait a minute," she said. "Sam, look at your plate. I know you don't care for broccoli, but I made that chicken specially for you the way you like it. Don't you feel well?" She put a hand to his forehead to test for fever. "I couldn't bear it if you got sick too. You too, Sara. You're not eating well either."

She noticed. I wanted to hug her and was angry at her at the same time. I'm like that a lot these days, and I hate myself for it. It's selfish, but I can't help it. She's so busy with Grandma, I miss her. I'm like this baby pulling at her and crying wah wah and she doesn't hear me. And the times when she does, I melt to nothing and get mad at her at the same time. What I think is that I'm a total mess, Miss Hasselbauer.

When Mom asked about Sam's not eating, he said, "I'm fine, Mom, I'm just full. Why can't we have fish for a change?"

I almost choked on that one. I know he was thinking of the cat, but after what happened Sunday it was so funny to hear him ask for fish.

I have to tell you about it. Last Sunday, a friend of my father's took us tuna fishing. Just the three of us. Mom stayed home, of course, with Grandma.

Daddy said he thought tuna was something that came out of a can. He was kidding, but I never thought of it as a whole fish before either. We were in a motorboat that zoomed way out in the ocean where it was rough. We could hardly see land anymore. Mr. Monomoto, my dad's friend, cut the motor and we sat there, rocking up and down and then sideways. He said it was a choppy day, good for fishing.

He took handfuls of disgusting-looking fish lumps from a pail and threw them over the side. I asked him what for, and he said, "That's to sweeten the pot, little girl." He laughed at me because I didn't know what he meant. I don't think you should laugh because someone doesn't know something, do you?

My father saw how I felt, and he told me Mr. Monomoto was throwing bait overboard to attract the fish to where we were.

I thought for one crazy second about helping myself to some of that bait to take to the lava field. Then, real as real, my nose was full of how it would stink up my clothes. They would have to throw them away the way they did that time when we went camping out at Yellowstone. I tried to pet a kitten near the bathrooms and it turned out to be a skunk. I was little then.

I looked at Sam to see if he was thinking the same thing. He was hanging over the side, and from where I sat he looked as green as the water.

The boat was rocking, and I didn't mind. I didn't feel a bit sick. The water sparkled so much it hurt my eyes, like looking straight into the sun. And when I looked down, the water was so clean and clear it made me wish I was a fish so I could live in it.

We waited and rocked and waited and rocked, and I

could hear the disgusting noises Sam was making. All of a sudden my father had a fish on the end of his line. He was sitting on a swivel chair holding on to his rod, which was all bent over. Something enormous was pulling us like we were a toy boat. Mr. Monomoto shouted orders at Daddy and was turning his chair this way and that. We were racing through the water. It was wonderful!

Finally, the man, Mr. Monomoto, leaned over with a curved pick and lifted out this big beautiful fish and let it flop into the boat. It was all silvery, and jumping around, crazy to get back in the water. What the man did was whack it over the head with a club.

I thought I would throw up, but it was Sam who actually cried out as if the club hit him instead of the fish. He can't stand any kind of violence. I know that from how he is with TV. Most things he can't watch.

He swore to me on the way home from that fishing trip that he would never ever eat fish again. That's why I nearly choked when he asked Mom for it at the table. It shows what he thinks of that cat.

Mom asked us, "Are you eating your lunches in school?" She looked at us both, back and forth, like she hadn't seen us for a while.

We said sure and sneaked a sideways look at one another. I know my mother caught that, because the corners of her mouth lifted and her nose crinkled up the way it does when she's pleased over something. She was saying to herself, how nice, my children are getting along so well together; they are friends just like I always wanted them to be. She was always trying to get us to do things together back home, but we didn't much. He was always like this weirdo I had for a brother. I don't really think that so much anymore, but here it's the cat we have together and only the cat. She doesn't know that.

Mom waved us away. "Okay," she said, "Mother's little helpers, off you go. Bert, you want to run over to the hospital with me tonight? Mother said not to, but you know how she is, she'd say that anyway just to spare me. Maybe the doctor will look in."

"I'm coming, Delly, of course I will. But there's no point in talking to the doctor until the tests are all done, you know that."

"Ummm." She was busy with her own thoughts again and wasn't there anymore. Bye-bye Mom, I thought to myself.

Maybe you want to know what we do with the left-overs. We put them in a grocery bag and then Sam hides it in one of the big garbage cans at the side of the house. After school, I pick it up, because my school gets out earlier, and we meet at the rescue rock.

The milk is another story. I found a whole pile of picnic stuff in one of the cabinets, so we use the paper bowls. We put some milk in a jar to take to the field and then pour it out in the bowl. Easy. Mom hasn't noticed a thing. We haven't gone on picnics since my grandmother came.

We see our cat every day but from a distance. He won't eat if we're close by, but he knows us. I think he can tell time, because there he is, at the rescue rock at about three-thirty every afternoon. I get there first, wait for Sam, and when he shows up, like magic, there's the cat. Don't you think that's smart?

He's so funny. He pretends we aren't there, and just parades up and down until we spill out the food and go away. We watch him jump down to it, and when we go back to the rock he isn't there anymore and neither is the food.

I'm so impatient for him to let us get close. I so want to pet him. Maybe he'll never let us and it will always be all one-sided. Just us liking him and being shut out like from everything else here. I said to Sam, "He's never going to like us!"

Sam said, "Take it easy. A cat like that, he has to learn to trust us. How do you think he got this way? Wild and on his own. People, that's how. Yeah, probably learned the hard way not to trust anybody. I know how he feels."

I don't know, maybe he does. Sam doesn't have friends, not here or back home. Not that I know of anyway. Why, I don't know, but he sticks to himself. He's elected himself chief shrink for the cat, like he understands him best. The funny thing is, it isn't that he likes our cat so much. He says it's just that he feels sorry for it.

I remember once my father saying that Sam protects himself too much. That was after my brother couldn't watch something on TV, like something embarrassing or even somebody in trouble. It doesn't matter what, because he was always doing that, leaving the room when something was on TV that he couldn't stand. I told you about the violence already.

I don't know what my father means by Sam protecting himself. I just don't think Sam has ordinary feelings. Look how he feels about the cat. He says he just feels sorry for it. How could he not love it? Mom says people are interesting to try and figure out. I do too, but I can't even figure out my own brother.

Today is what I want to tell you about. I think I said already that I get home first and carry the bag of leftovers to the lava field and wait for Sam. So today I was waiting for him at the rescue rock with plenty of time to think, which isn't a good thing.

I haven't told you about school yet. There isn't much to tell . . . it stinks. There's this girl I wanted to be friends with, but no more. Her name is Doris, and she's so pretty, like a little Japanese doll. Anyway, today she was playing double dutch on the driveway again with a bunch of others kids, and I wasn't even watching because of the last time when she wouldn't let me take an end. I couldn't believe it when she called me and asked if I wanted to play.

So I said okay. I was jumping in and out and doing pretty good. I love double dutch. For once I felt almost normal, playing with other kids. You all know me, right? Most of us started kindergarten together. But here it's like they don't even see me, much less know me. So jumping rope today felt real good, like I could forget that I'm new here. Know what I mean?

It's been hot the last couple of days, even though it's February. And maybe the best thing about going to school here is that I can go in my bare feet. Wouldn't you, if you had the chance? Well, we were jumping rope on this hot paved driveway, and I was sweating and the bottoms of my feet were getting hotter and hotter. But I didn't want to stop. I didn't want to ruin things just when I was getting started, playing with them and all. But finally I had to quit, because I couldn't stand it anymore. My feet were getting blisters.

I dropped out and said so long and practically limped away. Nobody cared or asked me why or anything. Remember that time my stomach hurt, Miss Hasselbauer, and you sat with me in the infirmary till my mother came? You got somebody to mind the class and you stayed with me. I remember that so clearly.

After art class I went to the infirmary to see the nurse. Mrs. Watenabe put some Bandaids on and told me I had to wear shoes until my feet get tougher. How will they if I wear shoes? I always wear my sneakers to the lava field because of the rough rocks, but otherwise no.

So I was at the rescue rock this afternoon thinking of this and feeling sorry for myself. Nobody at home would do that, not even ask why I had to drop my end. People are really different here, Miss Hasselbauer. Really deep-down different. I was wondering when homesickness stops, like waiting for a bellyache to go away.

Then Sam came. I asked him, "Where were you? How come you're so late?"

He said, "I walked."

"How come?" It's really a long walk from his school to our house here. He always takes the bus. It stops right at the head of our road.

He said, "Just some of the guys on the bus wanted some fun. You know how those jerks are. They want to fight, and I won't. They can't get that through their dumb heads. I loused up the baseball game for them," he added as if it wasn't anything. Poor Sam. I got all the athlete genes in the family.

"So what happened?"

"You know that kid, Eddie Nutt from the pet store? He was on the bus, at the back, only he didn't do anything. I mean, he wasn't one of the ones horsing around with me. Then, I don't know what really happened, but he must have started up with somebody at the same time. Next thing I know, there was a big scramble back there. It was a big help. I was able to get off the next stop, home free."

I wanted to ask him if he thought that Eddie helped him on purpose, but then we both shut up, because there he was, our cat. He was standing on the rock nearest us, just like that, as if he were beamed down. I could have reached out and touched him. It was the first time he had let us come this close.

His skinny tail swished and his yellow eyes were on us as if to say, go ahead, look me over, I'm doing you a big favor. Look me over if you want, but what I want has nothing to do with you. It has to do with what's in that bag. He didn't make any sound, no meow, nothing begging about him. He stared at us while we stared at him.

Sam moved very slowly. He emptied the grocery bag on the ground between the rocks, and I poured the milk. Out spilled last night's leftovers—chicken, bits of noodles, and broccoli.

This time the cat didn't wait until we left. He jumped down and walked around his dinner like he was at a party and was choosing what to pick. He went straight for the broccoli. Can you believe it? Broccoli, of all things.

I think I was holding my breath. There's something really comical about this cat. It's like he thinks he's something special and not just a stray cat. He thinks he's a king, only he's going around in this terrific disguise to make people think he's just a tramp.

He sniffed around, picking out pieces of broccoli until it was all gone. When there wasn't a bit left, he looked up at us, and for the first time I heard him speak. Except, of course, for the yowling when he was in pain. This time he lapped his tongue around his mouth and said something to us plain as plain.

I swear when he said meow he was really saying, "Any more?" Not "More, please," like in *Oliver Twist*, all begging and scared. No, it was, "Hey, any more of this good stuff? Get it out here on the double."

That's when I thought of the name. Plenty of times Sam and I talked about a name. I wanted Rambo, because that's who our cat was like, all black and fighting. Sam hates the Rambo movies and wanted to name him Prince, because he's like that too.

But when I saw how much he liked that broccoli, I knew his name. "Broccoli," I whispered loud enough for Sam to hear. He knew right away what I meant.

It was the perfect name.

Then Broccoli went for the rest of the food. He snapped and chewed until it was all gone. He isn't fussy the way they make cats out to be on TV commercials. Ours eats anything. My mother would love him, since she has to cook special for Sam sometimes. He only likes about three things—chicken, pizza, and peanut butter. That's it. He drives her crazy.

Then Broccoli hunched over the milk, lapping it up until it was gone. Afterward he washed himself. Absolutely, my mother would love him.

When he was done with that, he sprang to the top of the rock opposite. His yellow eyes were on us again, and I could practically hear him say, "The food is gone, so there's no point in hanging around. But first I'll give you a little treat." He posed for us with a lifted paw the way he did that first time.

I wish I had a camera so I could show you what he's like. Sam says he'll bring one and take pictures so I could send them to you. We could see he wasn't so starving anymore. His ribs don't stick out so much.

While he was posing I heard a loud noise like *clang*, like something hit a rock nearby. At the same time, our cat leaped up and was gone the next second.

Eddie Nutt was throwing stones again.

I could see him with another one in his hand. I yelled, "Quit that! You almost hit our cat."

He yelled back, "Oh yeah? If I was aiming I would have got him, bang, right in the eye."

We didn't invite him, but he came over anyhow. He saw the empty bowl and just nodded his head. "Figures," he said.

Sam was looking off someplace, whistling like he didn't even know Eddie was there. He can be unfriendly too, only not in the mean way that Eddie is. Sam is more like Broccoli, staying apart until he decides different.

Eddie and Sam look funny together. My brother is big and blubbery with skin that gets red not tan. Also, he has real light floppy hair, lighter than mine. Eddie is the opposite, small and all dark muscle.

He sat down on our rock and tossed the stone he was holding into the bowl. "You want to throw away good food on that cat? Go ahead. It won't get you anyplace. You'll never tame a wild one in a million years. It'll probably eat you first." He actually smiled at me. He was just teasing, of course, the way my father does sometimes, and I knew that. So I smiled back at him. It was like we were seeing one another for the first time. You would say "connecting," Miss Hasselbauer, the way you told us to for this project.

Eddie looks so different when he smiles. He has these white teeth and his eyes crinkle up and he's really not so bad-looking. In fact . . . Well, what I mean is, he looks nice when he smiles.

"Hey, you!" he said to Sam.

"Me?" said Sam, pointing to himself like he was doing a double take in the movies. Anyone could see he was being sarcastic.

"Yeah, you. You got off easy on that bus. Now me, I got me this on account of you." He showed us a long scratch on the back of his neck.

What could Sam say? He said, "Thanks," but he didn't sound like he meant it.

Eddie wasn't that dumb. He caught that, too. He said, "Don't thank me. I wouldn't care if they took your head off. Some kid was crowding me. I don't like that." Nobody was mentioning what Sam did for Eddie at the pet store.

But then, out of the blue, Eddie said, "Eh, you want to see something?"

We followed him. Close to the wall of rocks that keeps out the ocean, he was making a dam. Actually, it was a swimming pool, or at least it would be one when it was finished. You have to picture this. There's a piece of bare ground in front of the wall like maybe as wide as a sidewalk. Maybe a little wider. Eddie had started to build up a circle of rocks on this bare place so that it would hold in the water that spilled over from the ocean side. The dam would be like an enormous bathtub, big enough to swim in. At least a couple of strokes.

Eddie didn't wait for us to say anything. He left us standing there admiring it. Right away he climbed up the wall and rolled down one of the stones. Sam went over and helped him push and then lift the stone onto the dam. That's how we started working on it. Eddie didn't tell us to, but we did. I bet he let us because of what Sam did for him at the pet store. I notice that some people just can't say thanks.

The trick was to find rocks small enough to lift but big enough to dam up the pool. Sometimes it took two of us and even three. I don't know how Eddie did so much alone. It was hard work. I could see his muscles move around like they were alive under his skin. The sweat made him look like he had oiled himself like those bodybuilders on TV.

He lets us work on the pool, but he doesn't talk. There's lots I want to know about him, like how come his father doesn't like him and what about his mother, things like that. But he won't say. I know that because I tried.

The three of us were working on a good flat stone from the big wall. That's mostly where we were getting the stones for the swimming pool. Most of the other rocks in the lava field were too big and too stuck in the ground to budge. We were pulling and heaving and finally got the stone in place at the pool. We sat down for a minute, breathing hard and letting the spray wash us off. When a big roller comes in from the ocean side, you hear a big boom when it crashes and over comes the water. Our pool will fill up in no time.

We weren't talking, but there was an easy feeling there. We had done a lot of building in maybe an hour or so. Eddie leaned back on the stones and put his arms under his head, and I could see him smiling at the sky. So I asked him a simple question. I said, "Does your mother work at the pet store too?"

What Eddie did then was to sit up and look at me like he never saw me before, like we weren't working together two seconds ago. One minute it was all nice and friendly and the next minute it wasn't. He didn't answer, he just got up and started messing around with the rocks again.

Sam got up too. "Come on, Sara, we have to go home. They're probably back from the doctor's by now."

I had forgotten all about Mom and Grandma's doctor appointment because of the pool! They had been to see this doctor a couple of times already. My grandmother has to take some tests to find out what's the matter with her. We can't get her interested in anything, and she doesn't eat. I think she's tired out from working. At least, that's what I hope it is.

Hey, I didn't mean to get sidetracked here. Back to this afternoon and me asking Eddie that question about his mother. He was acting like he was mad at me, so I said to him, "Hey, I didn't mean anything." I really felt terrible.

He nodded but didn't look at me. He pushed stones around, being very busy.

I said, "Okay if we work on the pool tomorrow?"

He lifted a shoulder as if to say, sure, what do I care, do what you want.

On the way home I asked Sam. I said, "What did I say?" I wanted to know what was so bad.

Sam shook his head at me like I was pitiful. He said, "You never know when to keep your mouth shut, do you? Everything with you has to be right away. He didn't want to talk, that's all."

Yes, but why not? What I think is that there's a mystery about Eddie's mother and that's why he didn't want to talk. What do you think, Miss Hasselbauer?

Mom and my grandmother aren't home yet, so I'm telling you all this while I'm waiting for them. *Click.*

Click. This is an erase part. This is not for Miss Hasselbauer or the class or anyone. This is personal, for me only. When I talk out loud it makes it more real; it's not just thinking it.

It's dark here in my room. It's late, and all the lights are out in the house. I have the sheet over my head so nobody can hear me.

Something is going on here, and I'm really scared about what it might be.

When Mom and Grandma got home this afternoon, Mom was smiling and jokey and acted just like always, so I thought everything was fine. Grandma said she was going in for a nap, she was tired. As soon as she was gone, Mom changed like she took off a mask. Her eyes stopped seeing things and her lips pressed together and she looked, I don't know, strange.

I didn't know what, so I asked her, "Is Grandma okay?" Because I knew it was Grandma. But I shouldn't have asked. Mom didn't want me to ask her anything.

She looked at me hard and opened her mouth to say something and then just turned around and went to her room. She closed the door, bang.

Daddy came home soon after and then they were in their room a long time.

Sam was in his room, and when I knocked he wouldn't answer me. So I played jacks by myself and practiced this Japanese song we're learning in school so I wouldn't hear anything. There was crying not to hear.

Grandma didn't come out for supper, so Mom took her in a tray. When she came out again, the food hadn't been touched. I'm watching Mom all the time.

At supper Daddy told us that Grandma was going into the hospital next Sunday for an operation. Today is Monday. Only a week.

I asked what for, and he said there was an obstruction, like something in the way, and she needs an operation so she can eat. He said after the operation she would come home and stay with us.

"Until she gets better?" I asked, and Daddy put his arm around Mom's shoulder and said, "Yes, baby," and Mom looked down at her plate.

Here's another thing. After supper Mom and I were in the kitchen, and for no reason at all she kicked a cabinet so hard she hurt her toe. She hopped up and down and cursed like I never heard her before, never. I didn't even know she knew those words. And then, when she saw me with my mouth open, she started to laugh, and while she was doing that tears were running down her face.

So I had to cry too, without the laughing. Just seeing her that way. She tried to get me out of it, hugging me and smoothing my hair and saying, "Don't, baby, don't." So I asked her straight out what I've been thinking. "Is Grandma going to die?"

What she did then was whisper, "Don't even think such a thing." She tried to say something else but she couldn't and just went out of the kitchen.

So what do they think I am, a baby? Something is terribly wrong with Grandma even though they aren't saying. I have this lump in my stomach, like when something bad is going to happen only I don't know what it is.

I'm glad now that I told Grandma about Broccoli. We hadn't named him yet, but I told her. It was a couple of days ago when I came home from school and was going to the lava field to wait for Sam. Grandma was in her recliner chair looking out at the view as if she couldn't get enough of it.

She looked so . . . well, I wanted to give her something, so I told her about Broccoli. When I finished she took my face in her hands and looked at me the way she looks at the view, like she was memorizing me. She didn't ask questions about our cat or start in about minding my parents or anything like that. She never does that anyway. What she said was, "You love this cat, Sara?"

"Yes, more than anything."

She said, "That's good. Love a lot. All you can."

She turned back to the view and then said, "And Sam? What about him?"

I thought she meant does he love the cat too, so I told her I didn't know, he doesn't say. "He likes to take care of it though," I told her.

She said to the window, "Don't be fooled by Sam, child. The trouble with your brother is that he feels too much, not the other way around. You can depend on it."

Everybody has something to say about Sam. I don't get it. It's not what I see. All of a sudden, I'm remembering how it felt when Grandma had me wrong. I remember that she was surprised because it was hard for me starting these tapes. I know I hated that, her not knowing me. I know I can't figure Sam out, so maybe this time Grandma sees something I don't.

Well, I gave her our secret, and I'm glad now even if she didn't get anything out of it.

I'm going to send this tape. After I erase.

I dreamt about Eddie last night, but I don't remember it. It was really nice when he smiled at me this afternoon. It felt like he was saying, hey hello. Also, he doesn't have black eyes. His are more like caramels. *Click.*

Click. Hooray, mail! Thanks, everybody, for the card with all the names. I pinned it to my pink blanket so I can see it first thing when I wake up in the morning.

Miss Hasselbauer, I love your letter and the drawings you all did. The ones of Broccoli were real good, only he's not so skinny anymore. Thanks for all the ideas about what to name him, but in the tape I just sent you'll hear his one and true name. Also, I'll give him your regards like you say. You don't have to ask, I'll be telling you lots more about him.

I showed the drawings to Sam, and he says they are too nice. He says Mr. Nutt should be more hairy like a bear and Eddie should have arrows come out of his eyes.

You say about me being a natural leader, Miss Hasselbauer, and how that will come out in time. I don't think so. It's not like that here. It's better that I stay quiet. It's hard for me to keep my mouth shut, as most of you know already, but when I get excited and speak out or raise my hand a lot, everyone looks at me funny. Still, in a way, everything is easier here. I don't mean the work is easier, it's just that there's not all that trying to be best. It's not like at home. It's a big jump for me from there to here. Here I'm a nothing. I feel a million miles from everybody in class and always will.

Another good thing today besides getting your mail was that this morning when we were having breakfast Mom told us our Uncle Steve and Aunt Carrie were coming. She says they want to be here with Grandma. She has to have an operation. They'll be here Sunday, day after tomorrow.

He's so funny, my Uncle Steve. He makes my mother laugh more than anyone, so I'm real glad he's coming. And Aunt Carrie loves animals. I know that because she told me that she once had a goat and two dogs. Maybe we'll tell her about Broccoli.

It will be better here when they come.

This whole afternoon we worked at our pool—Eddie, Sam and I—in the pouring rain. We didn't care a bit. The rain just made it more fun.

It's funny about Eddie, because I wouldn't exactly call us friends. I don't know what we are. Ever since last Monday, the three of us have been working on the pool together, and today is Friday. We won't see him on the weekend, because he has to work in his father's pet store then.

Eddie piles his rocks and we help one another lift, but that's all. I mean we work together, but we don't talk much. I sure don't ask him anything after the last time.

Once in a while I catch him looking at me or Sam. Just watching us like he's trying to decide about us. Sometimes I think Eddie's the one that needs taming, not our cat. He's more like a wild thing than Broccoli.

58

He trusts nobody, Miss Hasselbauer, and at least our cat trusts us. He's beginning to, anyway.

I figure if I just stay friendly, Eddie'll ease up, like Broccoli. But I never met anybody like him in my whole life, so angry and suspicious over nothing.

Today, for instance. Sam and I were dragging one of the rocks down from the wall. It's really hard work, and the rain was coming down and we were both so filthy. Sam pushed some hair out of his eyes and left a big streak of dirt. Also, his glasses were so wet he could hardly see out of them. I had to let down my end of the rock because I was laughing at him, he was so dirty and blind.

Sam knew he looked funny. He said, "What I need is a pair of windshield wipers for my glasses." He flicked a finger back and forth in front of them and crossed his eyes. It wasn't anything, but we got the giggles anyhow. We sat on the rocks and laughed and got rain in our mouths.

So Eddie saw us, and right away he thought we were laughing at him. He was down working on the pool wall. He yelled at us, "G'wan home if you think this is such a joke. Go ahead. You think I'm a free show?"

We explained, but he didn't like it. That's what I mean about him not trusting. I really feel bad about Eddie thinking we were making fun of him.

Sam is usually the last one to get to the lava field, because he stops off at the veggie restaurant on his way home from school. That's where we get food for Broccoli now. I can just see you guys sticking your fingers down your throats every time I mention you know what. I mean broccoli. Sam sometimes holds his nose when he gives it to our cat. Not me. I don't like to eat it, but I love it anyhow. Anyway, we don't have to save leftovers anymore ever since Sam found this restaurant.

He saw the place from the window of the bus a couple of days ago. He said he read a sign on it that said, "Special Today: Broccoli casserole." He got right off and asked the owner if he could have what they throw out. He told about needing to feed our cat. Now the man saves us bits of broccoli and whatever else he doesn't want, and Sam brings it to the lava field in a box like McDonald's.

When I got home from school today, Mom was in her room cleaning out her closet. She never does that. She hates housework worse than anything, worse than I do. She told me once that one of the reasons she went back to work was so she could pay someone to clean for her. She's on leave now, but she was going to send in articles to the newspaper from here. Some of you know that she wrote the "People are Funny" column for the *Boston Star*. Well, she hasn't been at the typewriter once since my grandmother came, and I used to think it was attached to her, like a growth.

About cleaning, only when she's angry or worried does she do it, and we all know it's a sign. We keep out of her way then. Sometimes I don't know what's the matter, but now I do.

I said to her, "I'm going to the lava field, Mom." She knows about the pool, but absolutely not about Broccoli.

She was deep in the closet, so I didn't hear what she said. It wasn't, "It's raining out, don't go," or "Stay and keep me company." I could have told her I was flying to the moon. She's not thinking of me now, which is the reason I slammed the door. She didn't yell; she didn't even notice.

When I peeked in my grandmother's room, she was on her bed taking a nap. She already has her suitcase packed for the hospital, and she doesn't go in until Sunday. It sits on her dresser, and every time I go in to see her it reminds me and flop goes my heart. She still acts like everything is normal in our house, and so do Mom and Dad.

I got Broccoli's milk, put on my sneakers, and changed into my bathing suit because of the rain. It's the middle of February but more like July here.

Eddie was at the rescue rock, sitting in the rain waiting for us. He waits, but when we get there he acts like he doesn't care that we're there.

Today, when I sat down next to him, I said, "Howzzit?" the way I hear kids here say. Just to fool around, you know?

That got him to smile again, so at least he's not mad at me anymore. He said, "Haole talk," like he's disgusted and I said, "Pidgin talk," like I was disgusted, and then we both had to laugh. Did I tell you his voice is deep like a man's? Today I learned that when he laughs it's like a high giggle. The kind that makes you laugh back.

Broccoli doesn't show at all when Eddie is there, and Eddie knows it. When Sam came today with the McDonald's box, Eddie left us and went to work on the pool. Our pool isn't all that far from the rescue rock, and I could hear him grunt when he lifted a rock. Hey, don't you think that's a nice thing to do? Not to hang around when he knows we are waiting for Broccoli?

So Eddie left us, and from out of nowhere, there was Broccoli on the rock opposite, soaking wet and swishing his tail. His eyes were on the box that Sam was putting down on the ground. Then, the first miracle! He jumped from his rock to mine. He was right next to me. I could feel his fur brushing my arm.

I didn't dare touch him. I held my breath. I could feel every wet hair on my arm where he went by. Sam looked up, and when he saw him there with me, we smiled at one another fit to bust.

Broccoli ate and cleaned himself. The rain had stopped for a while, and he shook himself so that his ratty black fur stood up. What there is of it. I think if it weren't for all the bald spots and his torn ear, he'd be prettier than Princess Di. He has this snooty face that always makes me want to laugh. He doesn't have anything to be so snooty about. You don't laugh when he looks at you, though. He makes you know that would be stupid. He knows better than you.

Then—another miracle. Instead of disappearing, he stayed. More than that. He jumped up on my rock again and folded himself up right next to me, right against my leg. That whole side of my body felt him there.

I didn't think, I didn't plan, my hand went out by itself and smoothed him from head to tail. Sam sat down with the cat between us, and we took turns putting our hands on him, petting him. Broccoli told us he liked it, because he purred like mad. It was the single most wonderful moment of my life.

He didn't stay long, but it was a first.

Then we went to work on the pool.

This is all I wanted to say. About the mail and my uncle and aunt coming and my Broccoli miracle. I just came home from the lava field and couldn't wait to tell you. I have to take a shower now and get out of this wet bathing suit. *Click.*

Click. For nobody. No one. Only me. The lights are out. The sheet is over my head.

She goes in tomorrow.

Tonight, Grandma's door was open a little. I could hear her crying in there. When I peeked in, she was across the bed and making these choking sounds, the way you do when you don't want to cry but it's pulled out of you.

I ran to get Mom. This was the first time I ever saw Grandma cry.

Mom rushed past me and closed the door. I stood outside looking at it.

I could hear them. Grandma was crying and saying crazy things. I heard her say, "I want to alert the newspapers. I want everybody to know."

All the time Mom kept on talking to her. It was like so many times when I was on Mom's lap and she would rock me and say, "There, there, don't cry, I know . . ." Tonight with Grandma she was doing the same thing. Whatever soothing thing came to her mind she said. Mom wasn't upset. She sounded just right, except she wasn't talking to me. This was her own mother.

The crying and talking stopped. I heard her say, "Goodnight, Mama. Try to sleep," calm as anything. She came out and closed the door behind her. She leaned against it and closed her eyes and slid down the wall to the floor. She sat there with her face in her hands.

Then Mom was the one who cried. I was on the floor next to her and had my arms around her shoulders and we rocked. She leaned on me and cried like she was tired of holding herself back. Only, she didn't make any noise because of who was behind the door.

I licked the tears on her face. I said, "Let's make up a story about a tear licker."

She sat up then and wiped her face on her shirt. I got a small smile.

"Daughters," she said. *Click.*

Click. Dear Miss Hasselbauer and all. I haven't talked to you for a long time. That's because a lot has been happening at our house.

It's all changed now.

My Uncle Steve and Aunt Carrie are here all the way from Washington, D.C. Uncle Steve and my mother stay all day in the hospital while my Aunt Carrie takes care of things here at home. When my father comes home from the university, they go to the hospital and the others come back to the house. So my grandmother has company all the time. I haven't been to see her yet, because they want us to wait until she's stronger.

Aunt Carrie is just about as big as I am, but she has a way of making you feel she can take care of anything.

She doesn't talk a whole lot, not like me or my Uncle Steve. But when she does say something, you can believe it.

Like the other day when we came home from school, she told me and Sam straight out that my grandmother is going to die soon. She has cancer and the operation didn't help it.

I knew all along but never heard the words. Sam and I never talked about it, because every time I tried to he would change the subject.

We were in the kitchen. I could hear the clock above the stove. I could hear my heart thumping. Just then, the main thing I felt was scared.

She let us sit there for a while, tapping the ashes from her cigarette, letting us alone. I watched everything she did so I wouldn't think.

Sam pushed his chair back. He was leaving. He was all splotchy in the face, so I knew he couldn't stand to hear this.

Aunt Carrie didn't let him get away. She said, "I'm not finished yet, Sammy. I know how bad this is for you. It's a terrible thing I'm telling you, but it's not the only thing I have to say."

She was quiet for a moment, looking at the wall over the stove. She said, "I want to tell you something even if you don't understand it. What I think is that dying isn't the most terrible thing. The most terrible thing is to die alone and without love. You must know that isn't happening to your grandmother."

I heard what she said, but the words were like ping-pong balls bouncing off of me. Do you know what I mean, Miss Hasselbauer? What she said didn't go inside me, the words didn't mean anything. All I could think of was what's going to happen next.

Our house is changed now, and not just because my aunt and uncle are here. There's like a bubble around the grown-ups. Don't think it's sad here, because it isn't. Mostly they all talk like they are being extra careful to be nice to each other. But they're together, and I'm on the outside looking in. It's something like when I'm at the lava field with Broccoli, nothing else is important, nothing gets to me. I have my *Star Trek* shield up, and only Sam and Eddie and Broccoli are inside of it with me. That's how it is with them. They are in this bubble together with Grandma, and nothing else is important. The thing is, knowing about it doesn't help any. I'm outside of it.

Sam and I stay all the time we can at the lava field. We told Aunt Carrie about Broccoli. She gives us food for him, so Sam doesn't have to stop off at the restaurant anymore. She cooks you-know-what for you-know-who.

What I want to tell you about though, is Eddie. He told us a lot today. I guess he was ready, like Sam said. And I didn't start it, Sam did.

We were at the pool. Its sides are all done, and that was some job, lifting and rolling all those rocks to make that wall. It comes to about the top of my legs, and we tried to top it with flat rocks so we can sit along the edge. The main trouble now is that it doesn't hold in the water that comes over from the other side. If the ocean is rough, it holds enough for me to splash around in, but on calm days the water leaks out through the cracks. So we have to fix that. I search for little stones to patch in between.

Sam was stretched out along the pool wall nose to nose with Broccoli. He says they read one another's minds that way.

I had just dumped a pile of little stones out for Eddie to pick from when Sam said to Broccoli, "You have nine lives, can't you spare me just one? How about it, cat? Just one measly life?" I don't think Sam knew he was talking out loud just then.

Eddie was on his knees patching the stones near Sam, so he heard what he said. He said to Sam, "One lousy life isn't enough for you?"

I knew right away who another life was for. Sam said it out loud and surprised me and maybe himself, too. He said, "Not for me, for my grandmother. She's going to die. Hear that, Broccoli?"

Eddie said, "Yeah, well . . ." He got very busy pushing those stones into the cracks. He didn't look up, but he said, "So what, everybody dies. You say 'who cares' to yourself long enough, then you don't. Now, me, I don't give a damn if I never see her."

Sam asked him who.

And that's when we found out about Eddie Nutt. It was Sam telling about grandma that got him to talk.

He told us that his mother had run off with an old boyfriend three years ago when Eddie was ten. He said, "I don't know where she is and I don't care. Like she's dead, see?"

This time I couldn't stop myself. I said, "She left you? She left you behind? Just like that?" I didn't mean to show how shocked I was.

Eddie said, "Yeah," like I had asked him if the sun was shining or to pass the bread.

He had stopped working, and sat leaning against the

wall near Sam and Broccoli. I was on the ground facing all three of them, hugging my knees, holding myself in.

It was too nice a day for this. I could hear the surf crashing against the rocks. The spray cooled us off. The birds were diving around in the sky having fun, and the sun was toasty. Nobody should have such a bad story to tell on such a day.

I thought of his father and just said the word. Not even said. I more breathed it. Like this: "Your father?"

Eddie looked at me only once, but that was enough. His mouth said one thing, but his eyes said another. They were sad, and what he said wasn't. Which do you believe, Miss Hasselbauer? What people say or what comes out on their face? Eddie said, "Oh, him. Yeah. He hates me. Ever since, he hates me. When she left he started in with me. Well, who cares? I feel the same about him."

Sam had his eyes only on Broccoli, like they were hypnotizing one another. I thought to myself that if this was on TV, Sam would leave the room. But that's how wrong you can be about a person.

He said right out, "How come your father hates you? Why not her? You didn't do anything."

Eddie told us it was because he, Eddie, was like his mother, and not just in looks. His father told him that plenty of times. "Bad, like her, is what he means," Eddie told us, snorting over it like it was funny. Also, you would think Eddie was proud of that, the way he said it.

I asked him if there was anybody else in his family. Maybe his mother had run away from a whole houseful of little kids.

He said there was just him, though he has relatives coming out of his ears. All his mother's family are local people, which means they were born here. Most of them live on the Big Island in Hilo except for his Uncle Manuel and Aunt Rosita. Listen to this! Eddie is a little bit Hawaiian, a little bit Portuguese, a little bit Chinese on his mother's side, and Scotch Irish on his father's side. Did you ever hear of such a mishmash, Miss Hasselbauer? His father is Canadian and has nobody, no relatives. "He came here on a tour and never left," Eddie said. His mother was a tour greeter, handing out leis and kisses. That's how they met. "One kiss too many," Eddie said.

Broccoli nudged Sam's hand with his head. He was telling him that he wanted to be scratched. You have to wait for him to come to you. He tells you what he wants, and if you grab him or pet him when he's not in the mood, he lets you know. That's the way Eddie is, too, so today he was able to talk to us because maybe he was in the mood or because we waited till he was good and ready. Or maybe because he's beginning to make his mind up about us and trust us. I'll tell you something, though, it's hard for me to hold back. It doesn't come natural.

I waited for him to say more. When he didn't, I asked him some things I was dying to know. I asked him, "Did your father like you before your mother ran away? What was he like back then? Did he always have Princess Di?" Mistake. Too much. I'll never learn. Sam turned his head and looked at me the way he looks at fish for supper.

Eddie's lips said the word *father* like he was trying it out, and that ended that. He closed down. No more talk.

Broccoli had had enough of us. Maybe he had a date, or maybe a wizard called him, or he had to go back to his kingdom. He got up and stretched and was away like a streak.

Eddie watched him go and said in a disgusted way, "What a baldy." He still doesn't like our cat, and our cat still won't let Eddie near him.

Then, suddenly, he laughed. I heard that funny giggle again, like a girl's.

He said, "I can't believe what I'm thinking. I'm a genius and I didn't know it."

"What? What?"

"His cat and your baldy, that's what. My father, he's looking to mate his one and only, his Princess. Nothing but the best for her. He even has an ad in the paper. He wants her to have blue-blood kittens so he can sell them off and make a pile."

"So?"

"So don't you get it? We pass off your cat as a first-class number one. My father will get him and Princess together and then . . . Can't you see it? She has baldy alley-cat kittens and he'll bust a gut."

Sam now was laughing. "And how do we do that, oh genius? Blindfold your father? Or put a costume on Broccoli and pass him off as Superman?"

Eddie was full of it. He circled around, holding on to his head, saying, "Lemme think. Just give me a minute here."

Sam raised his eyebrows at me like saying, what do we have here?

Eddie stopped and pointed to Sam like there was a light over his head. He said, "That's it. What you said.

A costume! We fix up your cat so my old man won't know the difference."

I don't know what it was. Maybe because of talking about his family, maybe because of ours, I don't know. But we all got crazy. We started to plan like it was serious and we were really going to do it. I mean, we were having fun. Up to now we only worked together, or talked like I just reported. This was the first time we were just fooling around.

We decided that we had to get some fur and paste it on the bald spots. Black fur, white fur, it didn't matter, whatever we could get. Broccoli was tame now. We could hold him and paste on the fur and pass him off easy.

I said, "Like in *My Fair Lady*!" I remembered an old movie that comes on TV once in a while. There's this dirty flower girl who gets all fixed up so she fools everybody into thinking she's a princess or something. I saw the whole thing in my mind: Broccoli is all puffed out with black and white fur. I walk down the street with him on a fancy leash, and people stop me and ask where I ever got such a gorgeous cat he ought to win prizes.

Eddie wanted to play a dirty trick on his father. But I wanted Broccoli to be equal with Princess Di. I knew that he'd make wonderful kittens for Mr. Nutt.

Sam said, "Okay, where do we get the fur?"

With a straight face Eddie said, "I work in a pet store, don't I? I'll skin a couple of animals."

Sam said, "Good idea. How about that white cockatoo you have in there? Do you think your father will mind feathers on Broccoli? He wants an unusual cat."

We were fooling around like that when we heard this terrible noise someplace out in the lava field. What it sounded like was an animal fight. Awful howls and screeches. I can't even describe it. The first thing I thought of was our Broccoli. We never did see another cat out there before, but Sam always said there might be.

We followed the noise, jumping rocks, Eddie ahead of us because he's so fast. I kept telling myself it wasn't Broccoli at all, there are other cats in this world. But as we got nearer to the screeches, I could imagine him on the ground, torn up and bleeding his life away. What would I do then, without him? How could I bear it?

Then the noise stopped. It was absolutely quiet, like somebody clicked off the TV. We hunted around for signs of something, searching between the rocks. I was ready to call it quits when Eddie called us to come see what he found.

Where he was, the earth was all scratched up and there were bits of fur on it. I covered my eyes while Sam checked to see if any of it belonged to Broccoli. None of it was the right color.

Our cat is psychic and can read minds, because all of a sudden there he was, fat and fine, and twining himself around my legs. He came because he knew we were worried about him. I picked him up and hugged him and held him up in front of me so I could tell him to his face how glad I was that he was okay. I told him that he had given me a terrible scare.

Eddie was standing right beside me. He lets out such a whoop that I almost dropped the cat. Something had given him the biggest kick, because he could hardly get out the words.

What he said was that Broccoli wasn't a he, he was a she, and what were we, brain dead that we didn't know this?

Well, I don't have to tell you. We were knocked flat by the news. I don't know how to explain it either. I feel like such a dope. I can just hear you guys laughing at us. We just, well, we didn't think to look. He, I mean she, seemed like a he because . . . maybe because she was so full of fight. Of course, females fight too. That just shows how you can be a sexist pig without knowing it.

After we checked for ourselves, Sam said to Eddie, "Does this mean the wedding is off? No Broccoli and Princess Di?" And then the three of us laughed our heads off. What I'm saying is that we had a good time.

I have to keep saying it over to myself. Broccoli is a girl. Also, this was the best day we ever had with Eddie. *Click.*

Click. Under my sheet, only for me, my private self, my talk diary.

I think so much about Eddie. I can't understand it. I think about his hands. Lately, I notice boys' hands and think of them touching me, and sometimes I have to look away, and sometimes I shiver. It depends. It depends on what they look like. Soft, fat ones are disgusting. Eddie's are square and hard and so smooth you can't see the knuckles. His fingers are long, and he bites his fingernails. He doesn't know I look at him, and he sure doesn't look at me. He's my most secret secret. Broccoli is only secret from Mom and Dad. Eddie is from everybody.

How can I be thinking of Eddie when there's Grandma? I didn't want to visit her tonight. In my heart I was scared stiff, because I never saw a dying person before. I pictured her blue with her tongue hanging out, awful looking. Not my grandma at all.

I said to Daddy, "Do I have to?" I wanted to run and hide. Like Sam.

Daddy drew me close and smoothed my face, and I needed that just then. He said to me, "You're my big girl, aren't you? Of course you want to see your grandmother. We won't stay long. You tell her to get well soon and give her a kiss, and we'll stop for your favorite tacos on the way home."

What he said made me pull away. That was a lie, that part about her getting well soon. He knows she won't, but he doesn't say that to me. They don't tell us the truth. They say how we have to hope for the best and that she's getting along. They don't tell us straight out like Aunt Carrie.

Mom and Uncle Steve were still there when we got to her hospital room. There was this curtain on the side of her bed, so I didn't see her right away. Then I did.

She wasn't scary, but she wasn't Grandma, either. Yellowy eyes, yellowy face, funny smell. When I kissed her cheek, I took little breaths like sips. Then I hung on to Mom.

Sam went right up to her and took her hand and put his face on it. He held it there, bent over her like he didn't want to move.

Grandma closed her eyes and mumbled something.

I know Uncle Steve had been crying, because he was

all puffy. He looked around at us and asked, "What did she say?"

I heard her. She said, "Poor Sam."

I don't understand why she said that. And another thing I don't understand is how, when their own mother is dying, Mom and Uncle Steve can get into fits of laughing sometimes. Then the next second Mom could be crying.

Like tonight, after the hospital, we were sitting around the table eating take-out tacos.

Uncle Steve began telling us how this Japanese lady, one of the patients there, came into Grandma's room this afternoon. Without even saying hello or anything, she began to dance for them. She was in her bathrobe, and held a real fan, and did an old-time dance. When it was done, she bowed and left. He said he never saw anything like it. He said it was something out of a bizarre dream.

He got up and tried to show us what she did, using one of the tacos for a fan. He blinked his eyes at us over the top of the taco like he was flirting. He's not a good dancer, or maybe he was tripping on purpose. Mom got up to show him how to do it. Then the two of them got into a giggling fit over it.

I guess Uncle Steve was funny, but I didn't see why they laughed at that lady. I wish I had seen her dance. Most of all, how could they laugh? I was still so full of the visit, so full of the sight of my grandma.

Mom saw me staring at her. She was all flushed. She said, "Just letting off steam, Sara, don't mind us."

Is that how people get when someone close to them

is dying? I try to think about how I would be if Mom were there in that hospital bed like Grandma. I can't. It's like falling or fainting. I can't talk about it, can't think about it, don't want to say the words even to myself.

What I'm going to think of now is Eddie's hands. *Click.*

Click. Hi again, everybody. I got your postcard yesterday, Miss Hasselbauer, and I'm so glad the second tape got there okay. When you hear it, you'll know how my grandma is doing. Thanks for asking. I pinned the postcard to the wall blanket along with the other notes from you and the class. I hope it's all covered over before I come home.

Eddie wasn't at the lava field all week, and Sam says he wasn't at school, either. So yesterday, Saturday, we took the bus to the pet store. We thought we could ask Mr. Nutt about Eddie. We were worried maybe he was sick.

I stopped at the window to say hello to Princess Di. There's usually some people hanging around watching her.

She was curled up on her throne, asleep again. I think she's lazy, not like some cats I know, especially one. I guess there isn't much else for her to do.

She's so beautiful, I can't stand it. Now that I know Broccoli is a girl too, I'm more jealous of Princess. I told that to Sam, and he says forget it, our cat acts like she's beautiful, she thinks that she is, so she's even with Princess Di. I guess that's one way to look at it, but it isn't my way.

Inside, there was Eddie at the fish tanks, not sick at all. What a relief.

At first he was glad to see us, because he showed it. Then, right away, he stopped and went back to the fish, spilling out food for them, not paying any attention to us. I've seen him angry and also not, but this was something else. It was like he was only half there.

Sam asked him how come he wasn't in school.

Eddie jerked his thumb at a man at the counter, not Mr. Nutt. "Because of him," he said.

The man looked nice enough, a small, skinny guy in a baseball cap.

"Him? Who's he? Where's your father?" I wanted to know.

Eddie got busy with the fish again. "Away," he said.

I waited for more, and so did Sam. I guess we both knew him by now, there was no sense pushing.

Eddie looked over at the man in the baseball cap. "That's my Uncle Manuel," he said. "He fills in sometimes for Pop. He's okay, but he don't know how to handle the store like I do. Pop would come home and find a mess here. School's nothing." He moved off to the puppies like we weren't there.

Sam wanted to go. He told me that if Eddie didn't want to talk, we should leave him alone. But you know me, Miss Hasselbauer, I couldn't leave like that.

I went over and squatted down next to Eddie. I said, "Come on, what's the matter? Something is. Hey, talk to us, we're your friends."

He looked full at me, and maybe I'm imagining this,

but I swear his eyes filled up. "Can't," he said. "No time. Too busy today."

The store had the usual Saturday crowd. Mostly it was families giving the free entertainment to their kids. Eddie held up a hand to tell me to wait and went to his uncle at the counter.

While he was there, Sam and I went over to the Princess Di window, but we couldn't see over the wooden partition. There was a door so you could reach in, but I didn't have the nerve to open it.

Eddie came back and told us that he checked with his uncle and could meet us tomorrow afternoon at the pool. He said, "Yeah, something is up, but it'll keep. Tomorrow we close. See you, okay? So long, I got work to do." He had this worried look like he was thinking of something else all the time.

We said sure. Sunday afternoons are okay for us. Nobody's home anyway. Even Aunt Carrie goes to the hospital.

Sam knocked on the princess's partition and said, "Too bad we couldn't give this poor lonesome cat a thrill. I bet she could use one." He meant about mating Broccoli and Princess Di. I think he just wanted to make a joke before we left to get Eddie to loosen up.

Eddie did smile at that. He said, "Too late now, even if we give your cat a sex change. Di's mated already. A white Persian. The best. Never did a day's work in his life. Pop said it cost a fortune but he'll make it back."

Again I was jealous on account of Broccoli. Princess Di had a fancy boyfriend and would have gorgeous babies. I asked Eddie how long it took to have kittens, and he said about two months.

That would make it the middle of May, and we would still be here. I'm so glad. I really want to see those kittens. I'll be telling you all about them.

We left because Sam dragged me away. He thinks people should be left alone if they have trouble. I don't. When I'm feeling bad, I want everybody around.

We talked on the way home, and we both agreed it must be something about his father.

"Away," Eddie had said about his father. Does that mean Mr. Nutt had left him too? I was dying of curiosity and also half afraid to hear it.

So this afternoon we were at the pool a long time before he came. We kept looking and looking for him to come, wondering what Eddie had to tell us. Whatever it was, it wasn't good, we knew that much. Broccoli was with us, stretched out on the warm stones with Sam.

I went for a swim in the pool to stop the waiting. My brother never goes in. He hates the water. He says he's going for the Guinness Book of Records for being in Hawaii the longest without getting wet. Whatever everybody else does, he does the opposite. And it's not that he's trying. It comes natural.

The water in the pool only comes up to the top of my legs, but I can take three good strokes across anyway. If the ocean is rough, the spray comes over and I get a shower. Sometimes other things come over, carried by the waves. Mostly junk like seaweed or stones, even pieces of wood that I have to watch out for. It's like what you see at the water's edge sometimes when you walk along the beach.

Today it was calm. No spray. Also, the sun was burning a hole in the top of my head, so I ducked under a lot. I can swim the whole pool underwater.

When I came up one time, Eddie was there. He looked terrible, as if he hadn't slept for a week.

I just said hi, and climbed out and sat on the wall alongside Sam and Broccoli, almost dreading to hear what he would say. It must be terrible, because he looked so awful. I tried to be very patient, while Eddie drew circles on the ground with his toe, just letting us sit there, waiting for him to open his mouth.

Finally, I couldn't stand it anymore. I said, "Please, Eddie, come on. What's the matter?"

For an answer, Eddie pulled a folded-up letter out of his jeans. It was practically falling apart he must have read it so much. He passed it to me. "This was on my pillow last Sunday," he said.

I read it aloud. It was short enough so I can remember every single word.

It said, "Your mother phoned tonight."

No "Dear Eddie" or "Dear Son" or anything. It just started in.

It said:

> She wants you back. She lives with him in Tempe, Arizona, in a trailer camp. She said for me not to come see her, there's nothing to talk about, but there is. I'm going.
>
> Think it over. It's up to you to decide. I

know you want to be with her. I always
knew that. No surprise to me.

Stay with Uncle Manny and Aunt Rosa
till I come back. They expect you. He'll
watch the store.

So long, kid, see you when I see you.

Your father,
Edwin Nutt

That's it.

To tell the truth, I was relieved. It wasn't so bad. I
said, "Hey, great. Your mother wants you."

Eddie kept up the toe circles, staring at the ground.

Sam wanted to read the letter by himself. When he
handed it back to Eddie, he asked him, "What are you
going to do?"

Eddie lifted his shoulders. He didn't know.

That surprised me to death. "I thought you hated
your father, he's so mean to you. How come you're not
happy your mother wants you? Don't you want to go
with her? I don't get it." I really don't, Miss
Hasselbauer, do you? Wouldn't you think he would
want to be with his mother, since his father is like that?

Eddie started to say something and then instead
flipped over the pool wall and into the water.

I watched him splash around and shoot water from
his mouth. Just playing around while we stood there
with our mouths open. I was about to yell at him when
Sam put his hand over my mouth.

When Eddie finally decided he had had enough, he
came out, flinging drops from his fingers at Sam. Broccoli got some on her, and she raised her head to hiss at

him. She hates that. She says, "Cut that out!" plain as anything if I get drops on her when I come from the pool.

I know now that Eddie was trying to get his head together in the pool, because when he came out he was ready to explain to us.

He was explaining, but I didn't know what he was talking about. First he'd say, "Yeah, he can't stand me . . ." Then he'd switch to, "It's not that, it's her . . ." Then he was off on something else. "He just left. Like she did. Why didn't he wake me?" he said, and then quit that and looked up at the sky, shaking his head.

I felt so sorry and mixed up myself. Eddie's hands were balled up and his face had gone so tight, like he was lifting weights. Suddenly he seemed smaller to me, like he had shrunk in the water.

I was shivering a little even though the sun was hot. I pulled on my T-shirt, and before my head was free the words were out. I didn't think, I only wanted to get that look off his face. I said, "Hey, how about you coming home with us for supper? My mother wouldn't mind. I always used to bring friends home."

I didn't even know if my mother would be there. Also, our house isn't exactly fun to be in, either. But I said it, and Sam wasn't any help. He was whispering to Broccoli like she was the only one he was interested in.

One thing my invitation did, it stopped Eddie from trying to explain to us. He said, "You mean eat at your house?" like he never heard of such a thing. He said, "Naw," but he smiled a little bit. And surprise, surprise, Sam lifted his face from Broccoli and said, "Oh come on, you jerk."

Eddie said, well okay, he wouldn't mind.

He's in the kitchen talking with my mother right now. She said I was excused, meaning I should get out of there and leave them alone. If anyone can get him to talk more, she can. Oops, she's calling me. I'll tell you about it as soon as I can. Bye. *Click.*

Click. Here I am back. I just want to tell you about supper last night, because I understand now about Eddie and his mother. I knew Mom would do it. Some of my friends tell her more than they do their own mothers.

I was just as glad that Aunt Carrie and Uncle Steve stayed at the hospital. Eddie wouldn't have so much family to meet.

Mom and Dad were fine about bringing Eddie home like that. They're always at us anyway about bringing friends from school. As if we had any. I've been telling you about that. So it was a good idea, bringing him home. Maybe they'll leave us alone now about making friends.

Do you know anybody that puts ketchup on everything? I do, and his name is Eddie Nutt. We had chicken and mashed potatoes and string beans, and he asked for the ketchup. Mom told me to get it like it was something she forgot to put out. I almost got the giggles when he poured it all over everything, but my father gave me such a look I stopped.

I think Daddy was extra glad for Mom's sake that Eddie was there. To get her mind away from Grandma. When she gets interested in something, she starts playing with a piece of her hair, turning it around her finger. She did that a lot tonight when I got Eddie to tell about the letter and all.

Mom was listening and going uh-huh, uh-huh. When Eddie got to the part about his mother wanting him back, he started poking the tablecloth with his fork. Hard. All of a sudden, my mom asked him, "Are you angry with your mother?"

Well. Eddie looked at her like she slapped him. Then, like he was just waiting for the chance to say it, it came out of him in a rush. He was all choked and hard to follow, but what he said was, "She left me, she don't care, she don't want me, no good-byes or anything. One day I wake up and . . . gone, no clothes, no I'm sorry, no anything. She don't like me, she likes him, the guy she went with. Now she remembers. 'Oh, I have a boy someplace, I think I'll have him back.'"

He stopped talking so he could swallow a couple of times. I heard his fork rattle on his plate, that's how quiet we all were.

Daddy said, "And your father?"

Eddie was finished. He slumped back in his chair and said, "Oh, him. He don't want me either. Maybe he did one time, but not now. I know that."

I only listened up to now, but when he said that, I was reminded of something in the letter. I said, "Hey, that's what your father says. He says the same thing, that you don't want *him*."

Eddie just looked at me like so what?

I really didn't know what I meant except that's what happened with me and Betsy Lloyd at first. She's still my best friend, even though she moved away. I used to pass her in the hall, and I thought she looked away on purpose. So I did the same to her. I thought she didn't want to be friends, and she thought I didn't, and we found out later we were both wrong. Neither of us wanted to be the first to talk is all. Mr. Nutt's letter made me think of that. He says Eddie doesn't want to be with him, and Eddie says the same about his father.

But nobody would want to hear about me and Betsy at the table, so I said, "I don't know, I just thought it was a funny coincidence."

Sam had enough too, like Eddie. He said, "What's for dessert Mom? I'll get it," changing the subject.

Mom sent us both to the kitchen to get the pineapple. I could hear my parents out there talking to Eddie, but I couldn't hear what and I didn't hear him.

Before supper, Eddie had called his uncle and aunt to tell them where he was. My father had him tell them not to worry, he would drive Eddie home. So after Eddie and I did the dishes, they left.

When they were gone, Mom went to her room, but not before telling us that Eddie had to decide for himself about who he was to go with. We were to stay out of it.

Okay, I'll stay out of it, but only because I don't know how to stay in it. I don't know what to tell Eddie or what he wants to do. I try to think what I would do in his place, and I'm stuck. What would you do, Miss Hasselbauer? *Click*

Click. Private, only for me. I have to tell this or I'll bust.

I never knew a person could be happy and unhappy at almost the same minute. I think of Eddie and I'm high. I think of Grandma and Mom and I drop down like an elevator. Maybe I'm crazy, like Sam says.

Mom had to leave the table twice tonight while Eddie was here. I watched her go and wanted to run after her, but I knew she didn't want me to. She goes to her room, and then when she comes back her eyes are red, but she's okay.

Eddie asked me about it while we were doing the dishes, and I told him how sad she was about Grandma, and how my mother hardly knows I'm there anymore and how afraid I am that this is how she's going to be from now on. It just spilled out of me because he asked and he was so nice and so . . . listening.

All the time we were in the kitchen together was so special. Betsy and I have this game, what would you be if you were a flower or an animal or a tree. I like it even better when we play it about other people. I just thought of one for Eddie. If he were something to wear, he'd be silk. Before, I would have said scratchy wool.

He had a drop of ketchup on his nose at the table. I wanted to lick it off. This means that I'm going crazy for sure.

I'm going to send this tape after I erase this part. *Click.*

TAPE 4

Click. Hi, everyone. Here I am again with a new tape. There's two more left in the box and two more months to go. I wonder what I'm going to be saying on them. Miss Hasselbauer, remember that time we were talking about science fiction in class? I just had a terrific idea for a story. What if the rest of the tapes had my future on them already? There's me, my voice on them, telling all about what's happening here the next few months. I mean, I would be hearing my own future, wouldn't I? Wouldn't that make a good story? I have to think about that. What if I heard something bad?

I can look out into the garden now from this bed. I finally took down the pink blanket. I don't know why I kept it up so long. All your cards and notes are on my dresser now. I know them all by heart.

Last night, when I was leaning against the screen and listening to the noises, I realized that I never hear any crickets. I guess they don't have them here. Every once in a while I hear my gecko go gulp like a tiny frog. Her name is Mary Poppins and she lives on top of this screen wall. She's no bigger than my little finger and is the same color, only paler. When I first knew she was up there, I thought, yuck, get that lizard out of here! But now I love her. She eats spiders, and I hate spiders worse than roaches. I like knowing that Mary Poppins is up there. She's my baby-sitter.

Did I ever tell you they have roaches here as big as airplanes? Sam says Pan Am could sell tickets. He used to call this place Roach Ranch until Mom declared war on them the first week. She hates them even more than I do. We have to make sure no food is left out and what's not in the refrigerator gets wrapped up tight. I mean, even cornflakes. She sprays and puts powder down, so we don't have them anymore. When we first came here, we'd go into the kitchen at night and turn on the light and see the floor moving. Those are the small ones. They look like watermelon seeds running around. Nobody here seems to mind them, they're so used to them.

My Uncle Steve and Aunt Carrie went back to Washington last week. After my grandmother died.

I haven't wanted, I mean I haven't been able, to talk to you about that. Maybe you could tell I was putting it off, talking about my gecko and roaches. But I really want to tell you about the Memorial Picnic we had for my grandmother. I think it was the most special picnic that ever was, and not sad. Except for one bad part.

My mother didn't come home at all that last night. She stayed in the hospital, even though Grandma was too far gone to know anybody. Uncle Steve couldn't make my mother come home with him. She told him, "What if she comes out of it even for a second in the middle of the night, and I'm not here? I'd never forgive myself."

Early, early the telephone rang and woke me up. It was just getting light outside. I stood in the doorway and listened to my father say, "Yes. When? I see. Hold on, dearest, I'll be right there."

I knew my grandmother had died. I went back to bed and pretended to be asleep when Daddy looked in.

Aunt Carrie made me get out of bed. But I couldn't stay in the house, so I ran to the lava field needing to be with only Broccoli. I so hoped she would be there for me, even though it was early morning.

I think she knew that. Maybe she was even waiting for me. When I got to the rescue rock, I called out her name. Yelled it. And right away she was there, opposite me. Her long, skinny tail was swishing around, and she had those yellow eyes on me like she was saying, here I am, go ahead and cry. So I did. I told her that my grandmother had died, and when I held my arms out to her, she jumped to me and let me hold her. See, she gave me the feeling that she knew just how I felt, and that helped me.

When I went back to the house, Aunt Carrie told me that Sam wouldn't budge out of his room. I tried, my aunt tried, but he wouldn't even answer us.

Everybody came home soon, and we were all ready to sit down for breakfast. Mom knocked on his door, and all she had to say was, "Come, Sam," and out he came.

Mom wanted us to sit on either side of her. I had dreaded this time so much, and now when it happened, my mother was my mother again. I put my head on her shoulder, and whatever was missing in her was back. Her other arm was around Sam.

I asked Aunt Carrie about Mom later, and she explained it. She said, "Your grandma is safe now, beyond suffering. Delly was so terribly anxious and fearful for her that there was no room for anyone else. Not even you two, whom she loves so much. Now there isn't anything to be worried about anymore. Now there's just the grief. That's something different. That's for oneself because of missing that person so much."

They talked at breakfast about what to do that would please my grandmother the most. They decided that we would have a special picnic on a beach as a memorial. She would have loved that, they said. I couldn't believe it! I never heard of a picnic like that. On the same day that my grandma died? Have you ever heard of such a thing, Miss Hasselbauer?

Mom said, "We are going to have the best, the most delicious, the most elaborate picnic that ever was."

She wasn't crying at all. Uncle Steve was the one who had to keep wiping his eyes. He asked her once how she was doing, and she gave him this smile and said, "Fine. Numb. Blessedly numb, thanks."

We all went shopping together. Daddy said one of the rules for a Memorial Picnic was no cooking allowed. Mom wanted everybody to come to the supermarket, so we all got to choose.

We drove to the other side of the island. I haven't told you about Sunset Beach yet. That's where we were going for our picnic. We all crowded in Uncle Steve's car, because he said today we were not going to separate. He had rented a big Pontiac, so it wasn't too bad.

When you go over the mountain, it's like night and day. It's not so built-up.

There's a road there that follows the ocean. There are beaches all along the way where you can see people swimming or bodysurfing or collecting seaweed. Sometimes the ocean is blue or no color, and sometimes it's greener than grass. The mountains follow along on the other side, so we were in between the two greens. What I like to do is look at the little old-timey houses along the way and think about who lives there. I think how they can wake up in the morning and go outside to pick a papaya for breakfast, right in their front yard.

This was Uncle Steve and Aunt Carrie's first time on the other side, and they couldn't get over it.

Aunt Carrie said, "How unspoiled it is here. This is the way a tropical island is supposed to be."

Uncle Steve gets more carried away. He said he was going to find him a house and live there forever. He said he was going to get rid of his business, throw away his clothes, and be a beach bum.

Daddy said, "Sure, sure," meaning the opposite. We all knew how funny it was, because Uncle Steve loves fancy clothes and good restaurants with white tablecloths and watching the ball games on TV. He would be a terrible beach bum. Nobody was talking out loud about Grandma, but she was with us just the same.

I made my father stop the car because of the dancing. We were passing some kind of park, and there were some kids there giving a hula show. By the time we got out of the car, it was almost over, but we still saw the last part of it.

It was a school class with girls about my age lined up wearing long leaves for skirts and flower leis around their necks. They were hula dancing while their teacher sat cross-legged on the grass calling out the words and beating time.

I used to think that doing the hula was just wiggling your hips. But really what it is is telling a story with your hands, like sign language. It's beautiful. We are learning one in school, and I'll do it for you when I get back.

We didn't see much of it, and then it was over. When the class was dismissed, the girls dumped their leaf skirts and flower leis into trash cans. It didn't matter to them. They could get fresh ones whenever they wanted. They threw them away the way we throw away Coke cans.

When I saw all those flowers, I thought of my grandmother and her plants. "My old friends," she called them. Also, whenever we went to visit, she always had fresh flowers on the table, even in winter. So I had this idea.

I ran from one trash can to another choosing six of the best leis I could find. I piled them around my neck until they were past my nose. I could hardly see out. Also, I was fat with leaf skirts. The people that were still standing around laughed at me, but I didn't care. I smelled like a garden, better than a perfume store, and I knew what I was going to do with them at the picnic. *Click*.

Click. I had to stop to answer the telephone. Sorry. Anyway, I had on all those flowers and leaf skirts when I squeezed into the car, and nobody in my family laughed or said not to. Not even Sam.

Hardly anybody was at Sunset Beach that day, mostly because of no wind. The ocean was flat and it was a school day. If the surf was up, there would be loads of surfers out there and lots of people watching. It's famous for that.

Mom spread a fancy tablecloth over the mats and I piled the leis in the middle. The flowers were yellow and the tablecloth was lavender, and it was so pretty together. My mother said the table looked like an Easter basket.

Aunt Carrie and I decorated the edges of the tablecloth with the leaves from my skirts. We didn't talk about it, we just did it. Daddy and Uncle Steve set out real plates and cloth napkins, not just paper. Sam, I don't know where he was. I don't think he had said one single word all morning.

It was a beautiful day for our picnic. The sun was full out, but it was breezy, too. The sand was warm, not hot. Behind us were the mountains, and in front there was nothing but ocean as far as you could see. Before we sat down my mother looked around at where we were and said, "This is perfect for her. Only mountains and ocean and the blue sky for company. She would love it."

I think even if the beach was jammed with people my mother would have said the same thing. It was like we were all alone in the world, all of us together. Finally, I was inside the bubble with them.

We sat cross-legged on the sand, except for my father, who gets too uncomfortable. He leans or he kneels and changes his position every five minutes. He doesn't like to sleep out, either. Once, when Mom wanted us to go camping in Jackson State Park, he told her that it took mankind thousands of years to perfect the bed and he saw no reason to step backwards. He and my Uncle Steve are the same this way, but otherwise very different.

I went around the table putting a lei around everybody's neck. That was my idea. Dressing us all up in flowers for my grandma.

This is what we had to eat at our picnic: Crackers with cream cheese and jelly, cold lobster, giant shrimp, tiny meatballs on toothpicks, and cole slaw and deviled eggs, potato chips and chicken so that Sam wouldn't starve to death, let's see . . . peanut butter and bagels and doughnuts and chocolate chip cookies and passion fruit juice and champagne. If I left something out, Miss Hasselbauer, I'll put it in later.

All the time we were eating, somebody would start, "Remember when . . ." and then would tell a story about my grandma. After every story we would lift our glasses and drink to her. A toast, my father called it. Champagne tastes like sour ginger ale. I don't see how anyone can drink it.

I wish I had brought along this tape recorder so I could hear the stories all over again.

Here's one: My Uncle Steve was eating a pickle and began to laugh at something. It went down the wrong way, and he coughed so hard that Aunt Carrie had to bang him on the back.

"What's so funny?" she wanted to know, and he said, "I just remembered something that Mama did. Delly, I guess you were in school that day. I was just a kid, and one afternoon she took me to see a friend of hers. You remember Aunt Mae?"

Mom laughed and said, "Sure, she's the one who was so darn clean and fussy about her house she had plastic covers over everything. Mama's friend from the store. I hated to go there. I never knew what to do with myself. So, go on."

Uncle Steve went on with his story. "Aunt Mae wasn't home that day, but the door was open so we went in. Ma looked around that tidy living room. Not a thing out of place. You got to picture this. She's looking around and I'm pulling on her dress, 'Let's go, Mama,' and I see her get this devilish look on her face. Know what I mean?"

I never thought my uncle and grandma looked alike, but it was a perfect word for my Uncle Steve right then. Devilish. I never thought of it before.

He was remembering back to a good time. He laughed and said, "So Mama is standing in this perfect living room and she says to me, 'Stevie, let's rearrange the furniture.' And do you know, that's just what we did. She was inspired, full of energy and giggles, like some kid let loose in a playroom. We pushed the sofa and chairs to the middle of the room. We even changed the pictures on the walls. When we were done she put her hands on her hips and turned slowly around, looking at this awful mess we had made, completely satisfied. I remember her bending down to me and shaking my hand. She said to me, 'I'd love to see Mae's face when she walks in.'"

We were all laughing along with my uncle. My father raised his glass and said, "To Florrie." That's my grandmother's name. We all said the same and clinked glasses.

Mom was listening to the story with her mouth

open, her hand reaching across the mat to Uncle Steve's knee. She couldn't get enough of touching everybody that day. She said almost crossly, "I never heard this before! Why didn't you ever tell me? What did Aunt Mae say when she saw the room?"

My uncle said, "I can't recall anything more than that. I told you it just now popped into my head."

He winked at me and reached across to pull my hair. "You like that story, puss? What do you think Aunt Mae said when she saw that room?"

"She said, 'Help! Police!' I told him. "She thought it was burglars."

Uncle Steve clapped his hand to his head. "What a smart girl we have here. Of course. But you made me remember something else. Your grandma left a note for her. I can see her writing it. So no police. Hysteria maybe, but no police. Mama and Mae stayed good friends. Aunt Mae would have wanted to be here today. Okay, Sara, your turn."

I didn't want to. I didn't have any funny stories like that. The grandma I knew was different. She wasn't jokey, she was just Grandma. I whispered to my mother that I didn't want to, and she tucked me under her arm and said, "That's okay, my darling. Your grandma thought you couldn't do a thing wrong, so she wouldn't mind."

They got to talking about how alone with Grandma we all were that day. None of the friends or other family, her two sisters and brother, nobody else was there.

Mom said, "She didn't want anybody else. She told me the only people she wanted were already with her."

She leaned over to say to Uncle Steve, "You know

how full of secondhand opinions she was and how much she worried about what people would think?"

Mom began to sift sand through her fingers, looking only at what she was doing while she was talking. "What I'm trying to say is that all that was stripped away at the end. She didn't care a hoot about anything at all, except us, except . . ." She stopped to think of the right word and then said it. "Except love. That's all that was left. Back and forth, from us to her and from her to us. That was so amazing to me. These last weeks I felt so strongly how it joined all of us, bound us together. Didn't the rest of you feel that?"

Everybody said, "Mmmmm," or "uh-huh." We were all quiet.

My mother began talking to the sand, to herself, to nobody. She spoke so softly I had to lean forward to hear. "The doctor told me. He was a kind man and he told me. He wanted to help me when he gave me the terrible news and how short a time she had left. He sat me down in his chair and said to me that I may not believe this, but there could be a kind of beauty at the end if pain was gone and there was acceptance and love. He said that. A kind of beauty."

She made a noise that sounded like a laugh but wasn't. She said, "Can you imagine hearing that then? Such a load of you know what, I thought. I didn't believe it. They were just empty words coming out of his mouth, a kind man trying to be helpful."

She looked up then and said, "I believe him now. It was like that for me."

She stopped and pointed up the beach. "There's my Sam, poor kid. He's taking it hard."

I forgot to tell you that Sam hadn't wanted to eat. He had gone for a walk along the water's edge and missed all the stories.

Now comes the bad part. I was the one who cut the picnic short. I had something happen to me, Miss Hasselbauer. A catastrophe.

After the stories my father and I went for a swim. I thought maybe it wasn't the right thing to do at Grandma's Memorial Picnic, but Daddy said absolutely, Grandma would want us to enjoy ourselves, especially me.

The water was perfect. Some waves had come up, small ones. I was jumping over them when I felt these threads brushing across my legs and belly. Suddenly I began to hurt. I screamed, it hurt so much, like a hundred bee stings.

Daddy came right over, shouting, "What is it!" He told me later he thought a crab had bitten my toe. But it was worse than that. It was the worst kind of jellyfish, a Portuguese man-of-war, it's called. Terrible disgusting things that if you touch them or they touch you they sting and leave marks like whips. Anyway, Daddy lifted me up out of the water and tried brushing it off me, still thinking it was a crab. He carried me to shore.

I was crying. I couldn't help it. I hope none of you ever meet up with that kind of jellyfish. A lady from the beach came over and took one look at me and told my family what it was. Everybody was frantic, of course, because there I was, crying so hard and with these red stripes on my body, and they had no idea why.

The lady went away and came back with a bottle of meat tenderizer. I mean it. She sprinkled it over me like I was hamburger. The lady said, "I never go to the beach without it." Pretty soon the hurt started to go away some, so it works. I wanted to go home.

We packed up, and I spent the whole next day in bed. Daddy had a class to teach and Sam went to school. Mom drove Uncle Steve and Aunt Carrie to the airport, so the house was empty. I remember lying in bed and tracing the lines of red marks across my legs and belly, and thinking that they will stay on me forever and would always remind me of my grandma and her Memorial Picnic.

That was last week. Now the marks itch a lot. Sam found a *National Geographic* magazine about Portuguese man-of-war and told me about jellyfish that were twelve feet across. He said they could swallow a person whole. Brothers.

I wish I had something to tell you about Eddie. I think of him a lot. He hasn't come to the lava field since he had dinner at our house. Sam says he's back in school, but his father still hasn't come home. I wonder, maybe he'll bring Eddie's mother back with him. It's possible, isn't it? I told that to my mother, and she says I'm a romantic and too young to know that life isn't like that. Why can't it be, Miss Hasselbauer? *Click.*

Click. Miss Hasselbauer, I have to tell you something. It's about Sam and what he and my father were talking about.

Mom was fine at the picnic and even a few days

after. Then she started not to be. It's been a couple of weeks now. I come home from school, and she's crying or on her bed taking a nap. She sleeps a lot, and sometimes she snaps at me for nothing at all. Or else she gets teary over nothing.

Tonight at supper, for instance. Sam said he wouldn't eat squash if he was starving to death. Okay, so what, he's said things like that a thousand times. So what happens? Mom gets tears in her eyes. Any little thing can get her going. It's not like it was when Grandma was sick and she wasn't paying attention to me. It's not like that anymore. She's like the sleeping grass in back of the school. All you have to do is touch it, and it closes and feels like swords. Mom is like that. Only sad, sad, sad.

After dinner tonight she went to her room, hugging herself like she was cold. I went to lean against Daddy, who was reading the paper at the table. Sam was there rolling crumbs instead of clearing, the way he's supposed to because it's his turn.

I hadn't said anything, but Daddy looked at me over his glasses and mussed my hair and gave me a hug, because I guess he saw I needed it.

He said, "Don't look like that, baby. Your mother is going through a hard time just now, because it's just beginning to sink in. She didn't let herself feel too much before. It's better for her this way, letting out her feelings. You understand me? She'll be all right, just give her time." He smiled, but it wasn't a real one.

Now, this is the part I want to tell you about. Sam stopped fiddling with the crumbs. He spoke right up and said to Daddy, "If it hurts so much to have somebody die, then what's the point? I mean, what's so hot about loving? Why do it, if you feel so bad when they're gone? You might as well hit yourself over the head with a hammer." He was all splotchy red, and his eyes were blinking fast. The way he talked, I knew he had been thinking about this before and not just that minute.

Daddy put down his fork and pushed his plate away. He kept shaking his head, like he wasn't all that sure of what to say. That's not like him. He looked at Sam, he wet his lips, he leaned his elbows on the table, then leaned back again.

Finally, he said, "I don't know what to tell you, son. Why love if it hurts? Well, that's all there is. Love. The bottom line. It's a great world out there and lots to do in it. I hope you do it all, but without love it's nothing much. It hurts to lose the person you care for, but that's the price you have to pay. Nothing is for free in this life, I'm sorry to say."

Now, here's the thing. Sam said to that, "If that's the price, I don't want to pay it. It's not worth it. It's leaving yourself wide open. I'm not going to do it ever. You say that's all there is? There's plenty else. I don't need anybody."

My father groaned and smiled at the same time. He said, "Oh, son, you of all people . . ."

Miss Hasselbauer, what I'm thinking is, what if Sam is right? It's so scary to see what loving can do to you. I don't want to have my heart broken. The only thing is, how do you stop loving people? I can't help it, it happens to me all the time. Don't laugh, sometimes it could even be somebody on a bus, somebody I'll never see again. . . . Or it could be a teacher or my cat or just anybody. See what I mean? I'm not even talking about my family or my friends. It just happens to me all the time. Even if I wanted to, I couldn't stop. It would be like trying to stop thunder or breathing.

So what can a person like me do about this? I love loving, but I don't want my heart to break either.

What I wish is that Sam had never brought it up. *Click.*

Click. Hi, everybody. Thank you, thank you. Today is my birthday, and I got a terrific present from you and you didn't even know it. When I came home from school today, your big fat envelope was on my pillow. Seeing it there felt like Christmas plus a birthday. I tore it open and read every single one of the notes twice.

April 17, and I'm finally twelve. I've been saying I'm twelve for so long that it doesn't seem like anything.

My parents gave me a snorkeling outfit, flippers and all, and tonight we are going on a sunset cruise where you have dinner while you're sailing. The boat has lots of sails, like they had in the old days. One time I saw the boat pass right in front of the sun just when it was setting. It didn't look real. More like a painting. I've been begging my parents to take me on it, and now it's a birthday present.

Sam gave me his present in private. It's some catnip for Broccoli. He wanted me to know that it wasn't for me, it was for our cat. I can't wait to see what she does with it. I smelled it, and I don't see why cats go crazy over it. I hope she does.

You all want to know what we're going to do about Broccoli when we leave. I don't know, and I don't even like to think about it. Sam and I haven't talked about that yet, but I know we have to soon. There's the rest of this month and all of May left, so we have time yet. I know we have to find a home for her, you don't have to remind me. Someone on this island must want a wonderful cat.

You asked about Eddie, so I'll tell you the latest. He's back in school now, but he goes to the pet store right after. Yesterday, Eddie passed Sam in the hall at school and asked if we could come to the store, he had something to tell us. Sam didn't know anything more than that.

My brother makes me so mad sometimes. He has no curiosity. I yelled, "Didn't you even ask him what?"

Well, he didn't. He said Eddie was in a hurry.

So what? Wouldn't you have hung on to Eddie's leg and not let him go until he told you what was so important? Maybe it was something about his father. Maybe he was home and the mother was with him. Anyway, that's what went through my mind when Sam told me.

So yesterday afternoon, we practically dumped Broccoli. We fed her and gave her a short scratch and then we took the bus to see Eddie.

Of course, we stopped at the window first. Princess Di was restless, walking up and down in that small window space. She's usually sleeping on her chair when we see her, but yesterday I saw her in action. She just walked up and down and up and down. I noticed she was getting fat. She looked like she was carrying a bag of cotton underneath.

I said this to Sam and he said, "Know what? I think she's pregnant. Mr. Nutt gave her a boyfriend, remember?"

While we were at the window, Eddie came outside. He looked real nice, with tan chinos and a shirt I hadn't seen before. His aunt must be taking good care of him, because he was cleaned up. There's black fuzz on his upper lip, which may drive Sam wild. My brother hasn't even started getting any yet. Eddie had gotten a haircut, too, but not short. He has the kind of hair that falls right back in place even if he swings his head around.

He took my hand to pull me away from the store. I'm just telling you that because that's what he did. It doesn't mean what you think.

He said, "My uncle can take care inside for a couple of minutes. Let's find us a place."

Two doors down, in front of the Indian Bazaar, there's a concrete bench. It was empty, so we sat there, him between us. Whatever Eddie had to tell us, it wasn't bad news I could tell, so that was a relief.

He said, "I got a phone call from my pop. He's coming home soon, he says."

I said, "Oh, hey, is he bringing your mother?"

What I'm going to do is take a needle and thread and sew up my big mouth. Eddie didn't say anything when I asked him that, but he crinkled up his nose like he smelled something bad.

He said, "He didn't exactly call me. It was Uncle Manny he talked to. He wanted to know how the store was doing. So my uncle told him that I was working every afternoon and some other stuff, and that's when

104

Pop told him to put me on. The first thing he said to me was, "Manny tells me you're a big help."

Eddie was trying to keep from smiling. Just those few words. He told us that his father had straightened out some things and that he was ready to come home. They'll have a talk when he gets there.

"That's it? That's all?" I was disappointed. Just his father coming home? He could have told that to Sam in the hall.

"No. Here's the thing. I asked him, so what about Her? I was only asking if she changed her mind about me. And he says never mind, I should keep my shirt on, he'll let me know when he gets here." Now Eddie isn't smiling.

Sam picked at the concrete, looking down. His floppy hair hid his face. He said, "What do you think he means, 'Keep your shirt on'?"

Eddie said, "Yeah, yeah," like Sam had hit on what was bothering him. "Why did he say that?"

My brother didn't answer that, but I did. "Your father is only telling you not to worry, he'll be home soon."

"You think that's all?" Eddie said to me with his eyebrows up. He was relieved.

Sam said, "Sounds to me like he's saying, don't be so impatient to hear about your mother."

He got up and stretched and said, "Let's get a hot dog. Hey, is Princess Di preg, or is the easy life making her fat?"

Eddie then told us that the princess was loaded with high-class babies. So. For everybody who asked about Princess Di, that's the big news. How do you like that?

Miss Hasselbauer, I've been thinking about what you said. You wrote me that people are the same at heart. You say our deepest feelings are the same and it's only top layers that make the difference. Honest, I don't see how that is. I don't think the other kids here are the same as me underneath. I found that out.

A couple of days after my grandma died, I was in Social Studies and Mrs. Mu was talking about our social security system; you know, for old people. All of a sudden I had to cry, because it reminded me of my grandmother. I held on till the bell rang and then ran to the bathroom.

A bunch of the girls from my class came in. They were fussing at the mirror and horsing around and having a good time. I was in a booth waiting for them to go.

I finally had to come out to go to music, and they were still there. I thought I had finished crying, but the tears started again and all I had was toilet paper to mop me up. I went over to the sink to get some cold water on my face, and I heard one of them giggle behind my back and say, "Haole crybaby."

So where's the same at heart in that? Nobody came up and asked me what's the matter. I wouldn't tell them about my grandmother if they tore out my tongue. They are on one side and I'm on the other.

I have to get ready now for my sunset birthday cruise. This tape will be in the mail tomorrow. *Click.*

TAPE 5

Click. Hey, everybody, get ready, I've got lots to tell and can't wait to tell it.

Last night, I was here in my bed reading and I hear this scratching sound on my screen wall. It scared me to death. Then I hear this whisper. "Sara, it's me, Eddie."

He was just a black shape out there. I said, "What are you doing here?"

"Shhh, not so loud! I don't want your parents in on this. Sara, listen, can you get me something to eat? Don't let on, eh?"

"My parents are at the movies, so don't worry. Sure we have food here. What's this all about?" He had me whispering too.

He said, "I'm going to sleep out at the lava field, and nobody can know, get me?"

"What! Okay, I get you, but come on in. I told you, nobody's home but us."

He said all right.

I went to get Sam and told him what I told you so far. We let Eddie in.

Was he a mess! He looked like he had slept in his clothes for a week. It wasn't a week, it was one night on the sand all by himself. Yesterday he walked around town until dark and then came here. He said he had eaten only one slice of pizza all day.

I made him a couple of sandwiches, and while he stuffed his mouth he told us what was going on.

Eddie without his mouth full is hard to understand. With food in there he was even harder. One thing, he doesn't tell a story straight. You have to fill in or guess a lot. So that plus the sandwich had me telling Sam what he said, like a translator. Sam needs for people to make sense when they talk. His mind doesn't jump around like mine does.

I'll tell you everything I learned. Eddie's father came home day before yesterday. That was Monday. His uncle went to the airport to get him while Eddie took care of the pet shop. When Mr. Nutt walked into the store, he said to his son, "Talk to you later, kid," and started in with the account books right away. That's all. Can you imagine? After being away for so long?

"He hardly looked at me once," Eddie told us. "He can't stand to even look at me!" He was tearing bites out of the sandwich like he was mad at it.

His father let Eddie sweat it out, and then finally, on the way home, without any warning at all, he told him, "Okay, kid, pack your bags. Your mother wants you with her. I knew it would come to this. She has it all fixed up with the local school. So you're on your way. Your wish come true."

Eddie said to us, "He wasn't asking me, he was telling me." After his father went to bed, he snuck out.

He told us lots of things nonstop. He said his mother just sent for him like a package. She didn't write or call him or anything. She was married now to the new guy. She works the night shift at some restaurant, and the trailer has room enough for him. It was okay with his stepfather to have him live with them. His father told him he was all set.

By then we were finished in the kitchen, and he went into the living room, talking, talking. He couldn't sit, he couldn't stand still, he walked around the room waving his fists, telling us these things.

Once he stopped at our big picture window and looked out at the blackness. He said, "I don't want nothing from him or her. They don't mean a thing to me. I'll stay at the field tonight. The beach was crummy. I'll figure something out tomorrow. I'll show him. I'm never going back."

Sam got us some Cokes, and we got Eddie to sit down. He tossed himself down on the couch and leaned back to close his eyes. He looked so lonesome with trouble, and so tired. I moved closer to pick up his hand. It was cold.

Sam and I began talking to one another with our eyes. His eyebrows went up, and I knew he was asking me what we should do. I let him know that I didn't know. He was rolling the cold Coke can around his forehead to cool himself off, and I was almost as cold as Eddie's hand.

Sam said, "You don't have to hide out down there. Stay with me in my room. That's a better idea. I can shove over, or there's the floor. It's better than those rocks."

Eddie rolled his head from side to side. He didn't open his eyes. "Nothing doing. Your parents catch me, they call my father. Maybe he doesn't even know I'm gone. But I'm not taking any chances. No to that."

Sam was leaning back, balancing his chair on two legs the way Mom was always telling him not to do. He got up so fast the legs banged the floor. He said, "Okay then, if that's the way you want it. We don't have any sleeping bags here. I'll take us a blanket. There's some on a shelf in my closet."

I screeched, "What do you mean 'us'?" I thought I had heard wrong.

Sam said, "Us, Eddie and me. Not you. You have to stay home, just in case."

At this, Eddie opened his eyes wide at Sam. "Hey, you don't have to do me any favors. I'll be okay."

"It's no favor," said Sam.

I knew it was the biggest one. Sam would hate it.

"I'm going too," I said. I'm the one who would love it.

Sam looked at his watch. "Twenty to ten. The movies let out at . . . I don't know . . . maybe in an hour or so. If Mom and Dad come home and find us both gone, you know how they'll be. You want that?"

No, I didn't. One of us had to stay, and Sam had that stubborn look. I could see it was going to be me.

Sam was like a general, the way he was planning. He said, "I'll be home tomorrow morning before they wake up. They won't know a thing. Sara, you fill the thermos with something. I'm going to fix my bed up."

He went to get the blankets, and I followed him.

"You really going to do this?" I asked. I still couldn't believe this was my no-doing, no-feeling brother.

He pulled two blankets down. Now that he was out

of Eddie's sight, he didn't look so sure. He was really nervous. But he said to me, "I'm not going to let him do this alone. I'm going."

He bit his lip and blinked at me and asked "What do you think? Should we sleep on top of a rock or down in between?" See what I mean? He was nervous, but he was going to do it anyway. I had to like him for that.

I told him they should go to the rescue rock. There's a big space on the ground. They could stay there. "It has to be a lucky place because of Broccoli," I told him.

He told me I had good ideas sometimes. I filled the thermos with Coke and gave Sam a flashlight.

When they were gone, I felt really left out. I looked into Sam's room to see what he had done. His pillow was bundled under the sheet, and it really did look like he was there. Especially since he sleeps with the sheet over his head.

Then I went to bed, but I just couldn't keep my eyes closed. I would force them down and then they would pop open again. I couldn't sleep for anything and kept imagining what it was like at the lava field, all dark and spooky and exciting. Maybe Broccoli would be there with them.

Also, I was thinking about what Eddie was going to do. He couldn't live at the lava field forever. What about his father? Wouldn't he worry? Or maybe, like Eddie says, he doesn't care.

I don't know how long it was, but I finally heard the car go into the garage. My parents came into the house, and I waited and waited, but nothing happened. I thought they would hear my heart banging. Then everything, even my heart, got quiet.

The next thing I knew, the light was in my eyes and my parents were bending over me.

Mom was frantic. "Sara! Sara! Wake up. Your brother's gone! He's not in his room. Where is he, do you know?"

My father was just as bad, maybe worse, because I'm not used to seeing him upset.

I had to tell them. I didn't want to, but couldn't stand them being so scared.

At first they said I had to stay home. "School tomorrow and look at you. You won't be able to keep your eyes open." But I told them that they wouldn't know where to look and I did, so they let me come along.

I know I should have felt bad about telling on the boys, but I loved it at the lava field with my parents so late at night. There was a slice of moon, but it went in and out of clouds. Mostly it was just a fuzzy spot of light up there and not much to see by. We had rocks to climb over, remember. I held the flashlight, and I was the one to show my mother and father where to go. They couldn't have done it without me. In my mind someplace was how mad at me Eddie was going to be when he was found. Also, I knew Sam was going to get it. But I pushed all that away.

I led them to the rescue rock, and when they shone the flashlight down, there were the two boys. They were wrapped in blankets with their backs touching, fast asleep. In between them was Broccoli, also asleep.

When my dad saw the cat, he yelled, "Shoo! Skat! Go 'way!"

Broccoli's eyes flashed on like yellow headlights. Then they turned off. She was gone.

I was sure my mom and dad weren't paying attention to me. I jumped to another rock and called her back. She came, my cat. She crept into my arms because she knows me and she lets me love her. She was there to guard the boys, I know it. I sat and petted her while Mom was waking the boys. I tried not to hear the commotion.

Without the flashlight the night sky in the lava field was full of stars, just a little above my head. I was sure that if I stretched up my arm I could poke a finger through one. There were so many stars and so close, I got dizzy staring at them. They moved like they were on wheels going around and around.

Behind me I could hear the boys. We were about to go home again, so I whispered to Broccoli that I'd see her tomorrow and let her go.

I think I already told you that Sam is a hard one to wake. Even last night, getting up from the hard ground, he was groggy and had trouble keeping his balance on the rocks. On the way home he didn't say anything and nobody else did either.

When we got back in the house and could see one another, Eddie shot me a look that would stop a train. I gave him one back that meant, I'm sorry, what could I do? I had to tell.

The only thing Eddie said to my parents was, "Please, don't tell my father."

Daddy told him that he was sorry but he had to. He wasn't about to let Mr. Nutt go another night without knowing where his son was. He told Eddie not to worry his head about that now but to go to bed.

Mom put Eddie to sleep in Grandma's old room.

She gave me an extra pat when I got back into bed, so at least she wasn't mad at me.

I couldn't tell about Daddy. He stooped over to kiss me good night, but he said, "We have a little something to talk over, Sara. That cat. Was that the one you rescued that time? The wild one?"

I didn't answer, but I guess that was a giveaway, because he said, "I thought so. Go to sleep now. It'll keep till tomorrow."

There's lots more to tell, but I have to stop now. Suppertime. *Click.*

Click. Hi. This tape recorder knows me by now. It jumps into my hand every time I walk into this room. It knows that I want to finish telling you about last night.

My parents must have called Mr. Nutt as soon as we were in bed, because I heard my father's telephone voice saying that his boy Eddie was safe with them.

This is what he said: "No, I wouldn't do that if I were you. Let him get a good night's sleep and come on over in the morning.

"Yes. Yes, I'm sure you are. Of course, who wouldn't be?

"No, no need for that. Our pleasure."

Then he gave our address and hung up.

This morning the doorbell woke me up. I knew it was late right away. It smelled late. They had let me sleep, so no school today. Ha ha.

I got dressed and went to the kitchen, and there was Mr. Nutt and Mom at the table. My father had a class to teach, so he had left already.

I stopped in the doorway. Mr. Nutt didn't look up, but Mom waved me in.

I stood next to her and leaned. Mr. Nutt said to me, "You mother tells me that Eddie's a friend of yours. So tell me, Sara, why would he run away? Why would he do such a thing to me?"

He was so big and sloppy sitting there, with his eyes all bloodshot and full of water. I didn't know what to say to him.

I lifted a shoulder and didn't say anything. I should have felt sorry for him, but I didn't. I knew how he was with Eddie, what he had said to him.

Mom squeezed me and said, "Go wake up Eddie, honey. Tell him to come here."

I said, "Sam too?"

Mom thought that over. She smiled a tiny bit and said, "No, I think he'd prefer to sleep."

Eddie was flat on his back in my grandmother's bed. I poked him hard. When his eyes opened, I told him, "Your father is in the kitchen. My mom says for you to come right away." I got out of there fast. Whatever he was going to say to me, I didn't want to hear it.

I went back to the kitchen. Soon after, Eddie came in with just his chinos on. He leaned against the doorway and looked at the floor, not at his father.

Mr. Nutt said, "Eddie, Eddie, I was almost out of my mind." He sounded like he had a sore throat.

Eddie didn't answer.

His father said, "I had the police out looking. Manny, Rosa, everybody. I closed the store and walked the streets. Why? Can you just tell me that?"

Eddie looked up and said, "You closed the store?" He was surprised, anyone could see that. Then he started to say something to his father and stopped and started again. He was getting more choked up and harder to understand as he went along. I can always follow him, but I'm not so good at imitating.

He said something like this: "Don't give me that. . . . You don't care. . . . You don't want me around. . . . Your store and your cat. That's all you want. . . . I know that. . . . You want to get rid of me. . . . I just did you a favor." He said a lot more than that, but that's the idea.

Miss Hasselbauer, it was awful. I wanted to hold my ears and close my eyes. I couldn't stand to hear any more or see the look on his face. I felt so bad for him.

My mother didn't need me to translate. She understood every word. I thought what she did was heartless. She didn't give Eddie one bit of sympathy.

She rapped the table hard and said to him, "That's enough. You're not listening. Your father is trying to tell you that he was worried sick. You hear that? He said he was almost out of his mind over you. Does that sound like a father who doesn't care about his son?"

She pushed her hair back, and her eyes were big and she was all charged up. She said to Mr. Nutt, "Something is all wrong here. Did you know that your son thinks you want him off your hands? What is it with you two? Don't you talk to one another? He tells us that you want him with his mother, not with you. Now you tell me . . . No, better still, you tell your son, is that so or not?"

Mr. Nutt exploded at this. His arms spread halfway across the room. "Of course he wants to be with his mother! I always knew that, prepared myself for that.

The day would come, I told myself." He calmed down some and said to Eddie, almost pleading, "What's this about me not wanting you? It's the other way around."

Mom had to hold on to me. I think I shouted, "No, it isn't!"

Mom shushed me. She pulled me down on her lap.

Eddie was still standing in the doorway. What he said next to his father was clear as anything. He said, "You never asked me, Pop. You told me. You said pack your bags. You never said stay. Always, always I know you don't like me because of Her. That's why."

"You think that? That's why you ran away?" Mr. Nutt leaned his elbow on the table and covered his eyes with his big hairy hand. I could see a little bald spot on top of his head. He sat there breathing hard, like he was running.

He talked only to himself, like we weren't there. He said, "No, I couldn't let myself in for it again. Not twice. Her, then him. Push him away, I told myself. Don't risk it. Enough is enough." He kept shaking his head, like he was saying no, no, no.

I didn't dare look at Eddie. I was sure he was embarrassed to death.

My mother pushed me off her lap and stood up and said to Mr. Nutt, "You and your son have a thing or two to talk over, and I'm sure you want to do it alone. Stay as long as you like. Come, Sara, we have things to do."

They didn't stay. Eddie went to collect the rest of his clothes, and they left.

When the door closed, my mother leaned against it and said, "Whew! What a scene." She shook her head at me and said, "Don't look at me like that. You think I was cruel. Not sympathetic enough, right?"

She held out her hand to me. "Come here, Sara." And when I did, she said, "Sometimes sympathy doesn't help as much as a cold dose of common sense. Listen to me. What I saw in that kitchen was waste. A terrible waste. Mr. Nutt was letting his son slip away, and all because of fear. Fear of loss."

My mother held my face with both hands. She said, "Sara, don't you ever fear that. Don't ever back away from loving. . . ." She stopped, and laughed a little. She mussed my hair and rubbed my nose and said, "Forget it. You don't understand a word I'm saying, do you? Besides, look who I'm talking to. I'm talking to the wrong child."

If she meant Sam, he slept through the whole thing.

Miss Hasselbauer, I want you to know that I understood everything my mother said. *Click.*

Click. This is for just me. I have to tell it out loud, because it's too much for me to hold inside.

When I went to wake Eddie, to tell him his father was here today, he was fast asleep. I watched him for a little while, because I never saw him that way. His face was all smoothed out and his breath came in little hiccups. His lashes were wet and stuck together. Then he cried out something, like he was having a bad dream. I was about to wake him out of it, but he stopped. His face went soft again. His upper lip has a tiny bunch in the middle, like it's swollen. I watched him breathe, and I breathed with him.

118

I didn't push him hard like I said to the class. I sat down on the side of the bed and shook his shoulder just a little. His eyes opened, he saw me there, he smiled. He lifted a hand and ran his fingertips down my cheek. All he said was, "Sara."

In that single moment was everything. I mean, nothing happened, that's all he said, but that moment was full of . . . you and me. You and me. That's what it was full of.

I touch my face where he did. I think it shows.

I'll never my whole life long forget watching Eddie sleep. *Click.*

Click. Hi, everybody, here I am with the bad news. I told you my father knew it was Broccoli at the lava field. He didn't say anything about it last night. At supper we only talked about Mr. Nutt and Eddie. I thought maybe he had forgotten about it, but Sam said don't bet on it. He was right. Tonight, when my father came home, we had a showdown.

He called us both into the kitchen and sat us down like we were criminals. He and Mom started in.

Sam and I told them and told them how tame she is and what a great cat she is. We had to hear about how we disobeyed them and how disappointed they were in us and all that. As punishment we were to give them our word, blah, blah, blah. It was pretty bad.

I closed my ears and my head and every part of me. I heard them talk and wouldn't let myself hear.

I said, "No, I won't promise. You're awful. I love her. I won't." I don't know where I got the nerve, but I

119

knew that they could torture me, they could throw me into boiling oil and I wouldn't promise not to see Broccoli again.

Sam had his lip sticking out the way he gets when you can't move him. He wouldn't answer them even when they told him to. He sat there like a stone statue except he had bright red spots on his face.

My father lifted his hands the way you do when you give up. "Delly, we have a mutiny on our hands."

My mom was furious. "We do not!" she said. She's stricter than my father sometimes. She wasn't going to allow any mutiny.

I couldn't stand it. "Broccoli's all I have!" I was bursting. "She's my best friend! There's nobody else here!"

Whatever it was I said, my mother stopped like I had punched her.

She held her hand to her forehead and said to my father, "My fault. That's what this is. Bert, all that time with my mother, you know, all that absent heart-breaking time these kids were on their own. I thought they had . . . Well, I thought wrong. They latched on to this cat. They didn't have anybody else, certainly not us. The child says it's her best friend. Back home, she's surrounded. You know what she's like. What have we done? Why did we come here?"

My father now began to fight with her. "That's a ridiculous thing to say. We haven't done anything but put them down in a new place for a few months. So they're unhappy for a while. So what? They'll find out that you don't stay unhappy forever. That's not a bad thing to learn. And another thing. They are old enough to be on their own, for heaven's sake. What do you think they do at home when they are alone? They certainly don't pick up stray animals to keep themselves occupied."

"But there they have their friends, their life!" Mom said. I like it better when she's arguing than when she's teary.

"Sam? Have friends?" said my father. "Are you kidding? At least here I see him with this Eddie. He was out there sleeping on the rocks with that boy. If that isn't friendship, I don't know what is. Sam? Is Eddie a friend of yours or not?"

Sam actually opened his mouth. He said, "Yeah, I have two friends. One is the cat."

Mom and Dad thought this was funny. They held up their hands like they were surrendering to the police. What I mean is that we won, Sam and I. We didn't have to stop seeing Broccoli. The only thing we had to promise was that we would find a home for our cat before we leave. My father's words were, "I want you to start looking for a home for her immediately. You are not to abandon her now that she is used to being fed regularly and used to having human affection."

As if we would. It was the easiest promise I ever made. *Click.*

Click. Dear Miss Hasselbauer and all. We've been busy the last couple of days trying to find a home for Broccoli. I don't have any news about Eddie. I haven't seen him since last Tuesday, and today is Friday already. Sam says he hasn't seen him around. We talk about him a lot.

We still have five weeks to go here, but my father

121

wants us to start looking for a place for Broccoli right away.

So today we started on our own street. Not too many people are home in the afternoon, so we didn't get everybody. But you'd be surprised at how many people hate cats. Not one person even asked to see our cat first before they turned us down.

We practiced together, Sam and I. I was to do the talking and Sam was to do the sneezing. See, I was going to say, "Do you want a wonderful cat? We wouldn't part with her for anything, she's so terrific. But my brother here got allergic, and we have to. We would only give her to somebody special, and you're it."

We thought that would do it, but it didn't. Most places I didn't even get past the first sentence. They heard the word cat and they were already shutting the door. You'd think I was giving away measles instead of a pet.

There was this one man. He answered the doorbell with a little kid on each arm. He must have been happy for company, because he let me finish my whole speech. He was listening to me while one of the kids was sticking her finger up his nose. The other kid was just a baby, but he stank. Sam was sneezing like crazy next to me, and I thought, hooray, this is it, he's going to take Broccoli.

When I finished my speech, he held out both of his kids and said to us, "Sure, I'll take your cat. I'll trade you for these two."

Sam laughed and said, "Okay, it's a deal, but only if you throw in the car."

They thought they were so funny. It was a very discouraging day. It looks like it's going to be harder to find a good home for Broccoli than I thought. *Click.*

Click. Hi, everybody. Yesterday Sam stopped at the veggie restaurant to tell Fred why we haven't needed any more handouts for Broccoli. Mom lets us take food from home now. Sam told him our problem about a home for Broccoli.

Fred doesn't want her, but he told Sam about the Cat Lady. He said she's some kind of weirdo who takes in stray cats. Her place is crawling with them. She probably wouldn't mind one more. Sam got the address, and this afternoon we took Broccoli and went to see her.

We got a cardboard carton from the garage, and Sam cut holes in both ends for air. We found some screen mesh and stuck it around the holes so Broccoli could breathe. The reason we had to make the box is that the Cat Lady lives back in a valley and we had to take the bus.

I was excited about going, but also worried about how Broccoli was going to take being put in a box. I knew she would hate it, but they won't let us on a bus here with a cat. We had to fool the bus driver. I had a lot to worry about: the box, the bus driver, Broccoli, and the Cat Lady.

I was pretty sure she would love our cat, but maybe she was full up. Maybe Broccoli wouldn't like it there. I drove Sam crazy asking, "What if?" so much. What if we're kicked off the bus? What if the Cat Lady slams the door in our face? What if it isn't a good place for our cat? Sam got so he wouldn't answer me.

For the first time ever I wished Broccoli wasn't so

poor-looking. She's fat now, and no bones show anymore. But her fur still looks like a black ratty old coat from the trash can. And she's still so snooty and choosy. You have to know her to love her.

When she was purring in my arms, I explained to her what we were going to do. She has a way of looking into my face when I talk to her so I know she is really listening to me. I told her we were going on a trip to see a lady who likes cats. We were just going to look the place over. She wasn't going to stay. I didn't say that maybe we would have to leave her there when we go home. I couldn't stand to tell her that yet.

I carried her to the bus stop, and Sam carried the box. We didn't want to put her in it a moment sooner than we had to. When we saw the bus coming, we threw in some you-know-what to keep her busy eating, and closed the box on her fast.

I hurried to a seat with the box while Sam kept the driver busy asking him where to get off, showing him the Cat Lady's address. The driver didn't say anything to me.

Broccoli was an angel the whole ride, but when we got off, I was sweaty with nervousness. We were deep in a valley where houses are crowded together in between steep hills. It was like being at the bottom of a bowl. Nice and peaceful, I thought. A good place for cats.

We had trouble finding her house, because it was hidden in back of another one. We didn't need to check the address. I didn't see any cats around, but we knew we were at the right house because of the smell. I can't begin to describe it, but it was nothing to what was inside.

I rang the doorbell, and someone called out, "Who is it?"

"It's me," I said, "Sara Davidson and my brother Sam."

The lady inside said, "Lordy, Lordy," and then she said, "Primrose! Blackie precious, get away from that door!"

It opened a crack, just enough to see an eye, half a mouth, and some hair. "Get in here quick," she said, and banged the door shut behind us.

The smell was what hit me. I didn't know what to do with my nose. We were in a small room, and at first everything in it seemed to be moving. It was like when you have a dizzy spell and things go round and round. But all it was was cats. I never saw so many in my life, all different colors and sizes. They were on every piece of furniture. Everywhere I looked I saw another one, most of them jumping around or playing with one another.

The Cat Lady said she was Miss Irma Badger, and that was funny because a badger is an animal too. She was a tall lady, and old, and her hair had one side tucked behind her ear and the other side just hanging down straight. Around her neck was a cat. It looked like she was wearing a fur collar.

Everything about her was gray—her hair, her skin, her cat collar, her sweater, everything except her eyes. They were very blue and shiny. The sweater she had on looked like it was falling to pieces. I think she wore it like a toy for her cats to pull on. She didn't care what she looked like.

She said, "Well, isn't this nice? We don't often get

visitors, do we, Scooter?" She was stroking the cat on her neck. "What can we do for you?"

Then, before we could tell her, she said to Sam, "What's that in the box? Something for me?" She looked at it like it was a birthday surprise and she couldn't wait.

Sam said, "It's our cat. We want you to have her. Only, not right now. When we go back home, the end of next month. We thought you would want to see her first."

He didn't say all that at once. While he was talking, she said, "Pigpen, leave Mishka alone, you bad boy!" She must have eyes in back of her head.

Sam said some more and again he had to stop. She said to one of the cats who was meowing at her legs, "Rex honey, don't worry, she's in the kitchen."

Sam finally got out what we were there for. By the time he finished, the Cat Lady was shaking her head no.

I wasn't so sure that this was the place for Broccoli. She'd have plenty of friends, and the lady was nice and she sure loved cats. But it was such a closed-in house. I don't think she lets her cats go outside. Broccoli wouldn't like that. I thought of the big beautiful empty lava field that she lives in. What I'm saying is that I wasn't sure about this place.

The Cat Lady kept saying no with her head. Out loud she said, "Irma Badger, you need to be locked up if you take in another cat."

She kept looking at the box like it was chocolate and she wanted some. She said, "Well, just a peek won't hurt, will it?"

All this time Broccoli was quiet. I thought maybe she was asleep.

Sam put the box down and opened the carton. And then . . . it was like a bomb went off! Broccoli must have been waiting in there ready to spring. As soon as the lid was off, all hell broke loose. Excuse me, Miss Hasselbauer, but if you had been there, you would have said the same thing.

Broccoli shot out, and cats flew in all directions. They were all scared of her. She was wild, chasing them around like they were all enemies. She'd go after one and then switch and go after another. There was so much noise and commotion. So much screeching and racing around.

Miss Badger was yelling at her pets, and I was yelling at Broccoli, and Sam was dashing around trying to corner her. He got tangled up in cats and fell, bang, shaking the house, scaring the animals even more.

While he was down, I caught hold of Broccoli and threw her back in the box. I held the lid down and sat on it.

The room quieted down, and finally, Miss Badger swept some cats from a chair and sat in it. I didn't count, but so many cats jumped on her lap that it looked like a quilt.

She was out of breath. "Out!" she said while those glassy blue eyes stared at us. Her finger pointed to the door.

Sam picked up the box, and as we were going out she said, "Oh dear, hold on, let me catch my breath." One hand was on her chest, and she was still breathing hard. "I'm afraid I lost my dratted temper there for a moment," she said. "I'm sorry, your cat upset my family, and I can't have that. Besides, shame on you. Why didn't you tell me your cat is about to have a litter of kittens? Did you think I wouldn't know in one second? That was sneaky."

We were too surprised to answer. *Click.*

Click. I'm going to send them this tape after I erase this part. I don't want to always talk about my worries to them. I think I already have too much and Miss Hasselbauer won't want my Oral History.

What I'm thinking of is how are we going to find a home for the babies and Broccoli too? We couldn't even find one for Broccoli, and we don't know yet how many kittens she'll have.

All the way home from the Cat Lady this afternoon, Sam and I tried to figure this out. He says he's going to find out how to put an ad in the paper when the time comes. He says I should speak to the kids in my class.

I don't want to. I won't. They won't understand.

It was bad enough telling Mom and Dad about Broccoli. Now we have to tell them about the babies. I'll make Sam tell them, and I'll go hide under the bed.

I think so much about Eddie. He wouldn't go off to live with his mother without saying good-bye, would he? Nah, he wouldn't do that. So where is he? *Click.*

Click. Good news everybody, Eddie is back!

This afternoon we were playing with Broccoli at the pool, taking turns holding her so we could feel her babies move. Sam is so worried about what's going to happen to them that he misses the fun. Today when he held her he said, "There they are," like it was bad news.

I know in my head that they are going to be a problem, but mostly I think it's wonderful that we will have kittens of our own. I wish Broccoli would send us a message when the time comes, so we can see them being born. They do that with fathers, and I think friends count too.

Broccoli was on her side with her belly resting on the stones of the pool. I had my hand on her trying to feel what was going on inside, when behind me I heard Eddie say, "Hey, that's not potatoes your cat's got in there."

I was so glad to see him!

"Where's Sam?" he asked. He looked the same to me, back to his dirty cutoffs and worn-out T-shirt. I couldn't tell anything about what was happening with him and his father. I was dying to know but didn't get a chance to ask.

I pointed to the top of the breakwater wall where Sam said he was going to look for whales. That's his new thing these days. Save the whales.

Eddie climbed up to talk to him, so I had Broccoli to myself a little while longer. I'm teaching her how to hug. I hold her up and spread her paws on my shoulders, but so far she's not a hugger. She lets me and then says that's enough and twists away. She belongs only to herself, but I know she has a loving heart.

When the boys came back, they were still talking about whales. I broke in to ask Eddie something more important. "Hey, are you staying with your father or what?" Wouldn't you have wanted to know that first thing?

Eddie left off talking to Sam and just said, "Uh-huh, I am." I didn't get anymore than that, because then he looked at me with this funny smile and said, "C'mon to the store. You'll see something."

"Right now? What? What something?" It was four o'clock in the afternoon! We'd have to go home to get money for the bus, and I didn't know whether my mother would let us go. We weren't on our own so much anymore since Grandma. I told all that to Eddie, but he said go ask her. He wouldn't tell me what was so important at the pet store.

When we got home, I heard my mom laughing in the living room. She had company. They were at the dining-room table having coffee, she and a lady I never saw before.

Mom introduced us. She said, "This is Clara Pilapil, who writes a human interest column for the *Honolulu Bulletin*."

Clara Pilapil said, "Hi, kids," and gave us a smile so full of fun I melted right down to my feet. White teeth, white outfit, red lips, bouncy black hair, I tell you she was a knockout.

Sam looked at her like he'd been punched in the stomach. He had to wet his lips to talk. He said, "My mom writes for a newspaper. She's famous."

Mom put her cup down and made a face at Sam. Miss Pilapil just laughed and said, "Don't I know. Why do you think I'm here?" She sat back in her chair and crossed her tanned legs, and next to me I heard Sam grunt.

Mom rolled her eyes up to the ceiling and said to us, "Don't you believe that. Clara and I have a mutual friend back in Boston, so I called her, not the other way around. I told her that I do a people column for a newspaper too, so here she is, and we're talking shop."

Mom seemed to see Eddie for the first time and gave him a big smile. She said, "Well, look who's here. Nice to see you again, Eddie. I've been wondering about you."

Eddie smiled back and shook his head and lifted his shoulders and went from one leg to another. He really doesn't know what to do when someone is nice. After all that, he said, "Hi, Mrs. Davidson."

My mother said to him, "Tell me, did you and your father work things out? What's happening at your house?"

Maybe it's because of her job, but she can always get people to talk. I wish I could learn to do that.

Eddie said, "Yeah, we're okay. We been on Maui a couple of days, me and Pop. Just us."

Mom nodded. "And what are you going to do about your mother wanting you to come live with her?"

Eddie said, "We had a fight about that, me and Pop. He said I had to call my mother and tell her myself. No way was I going to do that. No way."

Miss Clara Pilapil was leaning forward in the chair, listening to every word. I saw her catch my mother's eye, and my mom gives her this look back that says I'll tell you later.

"So? So what happened? Did you?" my mother asked. It was like she was hearing the questions I was asking in my head and saying them out loud for me.

Eddie never took his eyes from my mother. This was between him and her. He said, "Yeah, I finally did. She did the talking. I was really sweating it out. Pop was right there, and he wouldn't take the phone. I just said right out, I'm staying, and I had to hear all these things about how she's my mother and misses me and all that. She wants me to come for a visit this summer."

He had to clear his throat, and then said so quietly I could hardly hear him, "It was so . . . I thought I forgot, but when I heard her voice . . ." He had to stop then.

Mom said, in her tough way, "Sure you'd have mixed feelings. It's only natural."

Then she looked at him like she was trying to decide something. I get that look sometimes when she's about to tell me something she says is for my own good and then I hate it. She said to him, "Eddie?"

He raised those black eyebrows.

"Mind if I tell you something?" She turned to her new friend and said, "Excuse me, Clara, this is important."

Mom reached out for Eddie's hand, and he stepped

132

up to her. She said to him, "Listen, I want to get this off my chest. If you saw your father that day he came for you, when he first walked into this house, well, you'd have to be deaf, dumb, and blind not to see what you mean to him. You know what I'm saying? What it was, this thing with you and your father, was fear. He was afraid he would lose you to your mother, so he tried to squelch how he felt. I only bring this up now because I want to be sure you understand that, okay?"

Miss Pilapil was watching Mom and Eddie the way my grandma used to watch her soaps on TV. "I was glued," Grandma used to say. I don't know about Sam. He was probably glued to Miss Pilapil and didn't hear a thing.

Eddie was looking down at the floor, not at her. His hair flopped over his face so I couldn't see it. He didn't say anything.

Mom lifted his hair away and looked into his face. "Hey, you mad at me?"

Eddie shook his head.

"Okay, then. Why don't you kids get out of here. Miss Pilapil and I have things to talk about."

I told her that Eddie wanted us to see something at the pet store and could we go?

Mom looked at her watch and wasn't about to let us. She said, "I'm sorry. Too late. What's so important, anyway?"

Eddie whispered something in her ear that made her smile. She said, "Why don't you tell Miss Pilapil what you just told me."

He did, and she showed that mouthful of white teeth again. Actually, she laughed right out loud.

Mom said to Sam and me, "I want you two back here

by six o'clock sharp. I hold you directly responsible, Eddie Nutt. I'll skin you alive if they're not home for supper. You and them."

It wasn't hard to guess what Eddie wanted to show us when I saw Princess Di's window. She wasn't there, but the window was decorated like a nursery, with bottles and rattles and even a box of Pampers in the corner. Mr. Nutt probably thought that was cute, but it made me want to throw up.

Mr. Nutt was at the counter. Eddie said, "Can I, Pop?"

Mr. Nutt wasn't too glad about it, but he said, "All right. But be very careful. I don't want her disturbed."

I didn't want to stare at Eddie's father, but I did try to see if there was something different. After all, there was a big change going on with him and Eddie. But he looked just ordinary. Didn't smile, didn't say hello son or anything. I was disappointed.

Eddie opened the little door to the window and had us peek inside the castle. It was dark in there, so he used a flashlight.

On a blanket was the princess and two new kittens. Just tiny little balls of white cotton. I couldn't stand it. I was dying to hold them, but they were nursing, and Mr. Nutt said you don't pull them away from their mother.

He had come over to where we were and stood by looking pleased as anything over what his cat had done.

All I could think of was Broccoli. I poked Sam, and he was thinking of her too, because right away he said to Mr. Nutt, "We have a cat too, and she's going to have kittens just like yours. I mean, they won't exactly look like yours, but . . . Wouldn't you like another cat, Mr. Nutt? We'll let you have the kittens for free. See, we go home at the end of this month and can't take her."

I got in there too. I told him that Broccoli was a wonderful pet and her kittens would be super.

Mr. Nutt just laughed it off. He wouldn't even talk about it. He kept looking in at his Princess Di and her babies, shaking his head and saying no, no, no, in a jokey way, like we were asking for something silly.

Sam asked him if he knew anybody who would want our kittens.

"I'll tell you what I'll do," Mr. Nutt said. "If a customer asks, I'll give them your number. What kind of cat is she?"

We had to tell him we didn't know, and that she was wild once but is very tame now.

This made it all different. Nothing was funny anymore. He said, "You got hold of a wild one? Those cats! They'll take over the island someday if they're not cleaned out. I wouldn't recommend that kind of cat to a customer. You know the biggest favor you could do those kittens?"

Sam and I both said, "What?" at the same time.

"Drown 'em," Mr. Nutt said.

And to think that I felt sorry for him once. *Click.*

Click. Hi, everybody. If I sound happy, it's because I am. I look around this little room of mine and I love it. I love everything I see, my lopsided bureau, all the leaves brushing my screen wall, Mary Poppins up there, everything. I try to remember what it feels like to be unhappy, and I can't. When I think of all the complaining I've done on these tapes I've been sending to you, it's hard to believe I'm the same person. I'm dying to tell you why I'm feeling so good all of a sudden, but I'm going to string it out, like eating a sundae and saving the cherry for last.

This afternoon Broccoli didn't come when Sam and I got to the rescue rock. It was the first time in ages that happened.

Sam said, "Maybe she went off with her boyfriend," as if it would be a big joke. Never mind, he was worried too.

We began calling and searching the place, looking first around the pool. Maybe she was asleep. I know she goes there a lot, and I don't like it when we're not there. I don't think it's safe. I think, what if she falls in, even though I know that's silly.

Sam and I separated and started jumping the rocks looking for her. Sam searched the part of the lava field closest to the ocean, and I took the back part, closer to where the houses start. See, once you pass the last house along our road, there are some low green bushes, and then the lava rocks start. It was when I was searching around these rocks near the bushes that I heard Broccoli calling me. The way she goes, it's not exactly a meow, more like a cry. More like, hey, here I am.

She was in between two big rocks. Broccoli was on her side, looking up at me, nursing her kittens! Five of them, five tiny wonderful black furry babies.

I couldn't count them at first, because the rock that

Broccoli was under made a kind of cave. I had to get down on my knees to peek in. When she saw me, she blinked her yellow eyes and made her funny meow again, only this time she said, look what I did.

I can't tell you what a feeling that was when I first saw our cat and her babies. I'm still flying—as you know.

I yelled for Sam. He took one look and ran home for his camera.

I sat there looking in at them, talking to Broccoli and waiting for her to finish feeding them. I had her food and milk with me, and I was so glad we had a can of her favorite. Oh, hey, she isn't so crazy about broccoli anymore. It's spaghetti she really goes for now. But we aren't going to change her name.

Sam didn't want to use his flash, because he said it might scare Broccoli. I told him that was silly, nothing in the world would scare her, but he wouldn't do it.

Pretty soon she came out, and while she was eating, Sam took pictures. It was a windy day, so her fur rumpled up and looked thicker than it was. She was beautiful.

While he was doing that, I reached in and picked up one of the kittens. I held it to my cheek and felt its little heart beating under my fingers. It wasn't all black, but almost. Its eyes weren't opened yet, but there was a circle of gray around one of them. Like a patch.

"Hello, Patch," I said. Its whole body fit into the palm of my hand, a little warm lump. I stroked its tiny head with the tip of my finger. I feel sorry for anybody in the world who hasn't held a newborn kitten.

We took all the babies out from the cave so that Sam could take some pictures of them too. We put them on top of the warm rock for just a few minutes. We put them down close to Broccoli, but she didn't look at them much. I hope she's going to be a good mother. You can never tell with her.

I can't wait to show them to Eddie. Last week was his turn to show off his kittens. This week is ours. Sam's going to tell him at school that he has to come to the field, we have something to show him and we won't tell him what. Isn't it great about Broccoli? *Click.*

Click. I shut this off and then turned it right back on again, because I didn't tell you about getting your mail. Broccoli's babies just chased it out of my mind. It's not that I don't love hearing from you. Honest, you wouldn't believe how I read the letters over and over. Everything you asked I already told you on a tape.

Miss Hasselbauer, I was really worried about getting too personal on this Oral History. You said to put everything down and be observant and all, but I thought maybe I put in too much personal stuff. Like you said in one of your letters, my brother Sam is a holder-in and I'm what you call a blurter.

So what I'm saying is that it makes me feel wonderful that you approve of my tapes and that I'm still part of the Oral History project. It makes me feel that I'm still in your class, and it doesn't matter so much that I'm such a flop here.

I told my parents that you would like us each to make a book from our tapes. Print it out and bind it

and all. That would be . . . I don't know how to say . . .
so super. A real book of my own. Sure, I'll be thinking
of a title. I asked Sam, and he said, "What about calling
it *The Broccoli Tapes*? He says that's probably all I
talked about anyhow. That's how much he knows.
Click.

Click. Yesterday was the worst day of my life. I didn't
know that when people talk about having a broken
heart, that it's true. That's what it feels like inside. My
heart hurts. Everything hurts, even my bones.

I'm going to keep this date, May 7, as an anniversary,
and I will never forget it as long as I live.

The kittens are in a box in the kitchen, and I have
my alarm set to wake me at two o'clock so I can feed
them.

It helps to talk. I know Miss Hasselbauer and the
rest of the class will be listening to this, but it doesn't
matter. I don't care who listens. Broccoli is dead, that's
all that matters.

All week we've been going to the nursery rock right
after school. That's what we called it. Broccoli was
almost always there with her babies. If she wasn't, she
would show up right away. First she would say hello to
me, twisting around my legs, wanting to be petted
more than ever. Then she would go right in, checking
up on the kittens. I think she liked being a mother
after all.

Yesterday, she wasn't with her babies and she didn't
come. Even after Sam came with food, she didn't
come.

I have to get over this part fast. Everything that happened from then on is like a slow-motion picture in my brain. I want to speed it up and tell every single thing at the same time.

We began calling and jumping rocks and stopping to listen and looking around. I was at the far end of the field and Sam was hunting around near the pool.

The trade winds were blowing just enough to cool off my skin. It was one of those days I can't describe, it was so beautiful. The ocean and the rocks were full of sun, and everywhere I looked was shiny.

I never looked at sky much before. I mean, when I was home in Boston. But I do here, because there's so much of it and so much going on up there. Always there are lots of clouds, and they make pictures that just drift off and form something else. Yesterday was like that.

I could hear the birds and the noise of the waves against the seawall. I could smell the heat on the rocks. It started to rain. The sun was still out, and it was the soft kind of rain I love. More like a mist. I knew if I put my back to the sun I might see a rainbow, and, Miss Hasselbauer, that's what I was doing when I heard Sam's terrible yell.

I don't remember a thing about how I got to the pool. Sam was wading out of it with Broccoli in his arms.

Funny how some things don't get real until after. It felt like pins and needles in my face and fingers, but I didn't cry. Just everything stopped, my breath, my heart, my hearing, everything. At the same time I saw better. Sam in the pool where he never goes, his mouth wide open and his eyes staring, Broccoli dead in his arms.

He laid her down on the stones. After a while I think I whispered, "What happened to her?"

Sam's nose was running. He didn't know. Then he said, "Maybe a wave."

I looked up at the seawall. It was a calm day, but in my head I saw the wall of water shoot up over and land on Broccoli stretched out on the stones. I saw it knock her into the water. "Swim!" I ordered her, but she couldn't, she was out cold. In the wave I imagined I saw a piece of board. It had hit her hard.

I looked for it in the pool. On the bottom I could see stones that weren't there before. Floating on top was some seaweed and a plastic bottle. We always had to clear the junk out. I didn't see any pieces of wood, but I didn't look hard. I didn't want to see it.

The next thing Sam said was, "We have to take them home."

He meant the kittens, of course. We didn't have to talk about it, we knew it and had to.

I wasn't about to leave Broccoli. Aunt Carrie had said the worst thing was to die alone without love. So the worst thing had happened to Broccoli. I wasn't going to leave her there on the stones by herself.

Sam made me. He said we would come right back, but first we had to feed the kittens or they would surely die.

On the way home, carrying my two in my arms, the tears must have started without me knowing it. When we walked in the house, Mom was in the dining room at her typewriter. Daddy was in their bedroom.

He came out in a hurry when he heard Mom cry out,

"What's the matter!" I don't think she noticed the kittens at first. She just saw us.

We told them.

Daddy said we had to find a box for the kittens, and Sam said we had one. Broccoli's box was under his bed.

Mom lined it with cloths, and we put the kittens down. They were making little crying noises like peeps and crawling over one another.

Mom got an eyedropper from the bathroom and heated up some milk. She seemed to know just what to do.

Sam and I didn't stay. He got a shovel from the garage. Daddy asked him what he was going to do with it, and Sam told him we were going to bury Broccoli in the lava field.

Daddy said, "You can't do that. The earth isn't soft enough. You'll strike rock right away."

Sam said, "We'll do it." And that was that.

My dad said, "Want me to help?"

He didn't know Broccoli, so we said no.

Daddy was right. We wanted to bury her at the rescue rock, but Sam struck rock at the first dig.

I was holding Broccoli in my arms. She was wrapped up in my pink blanket. I just took it from home and didn't ask.

I waited at the rescue rock with her while Sam tried to find a place he could dig. I saw him try at the nursery rock. That would have been right. I wanted her to be in a place that meant something to us. I watched him give up and dig other places. One thing we know: Broccoli was going to be buried there, at the lava field.

Finally, I saw him dig where the bushes were. It was

near the nursery rock. Broccoli must have wandered around there lots of times. As I carried her there, I told myself it might have been her favorite place.

We put her down and piled the dirt over and then gathered stones and covered her with pieces of lava rock.

Sam wanted to go right home, but I couldn't leave yet. I wanted something, some kind of ceremony like a real funeral.

I said, "You don't have to do anything, but stay here for just a little while, okay?" I was remembering how my mom was that day at Grandma's picnic, and how she only wanted us with her, the ones who knew and loved Grandma.

That's why I wanted Sam to stay. He was the only other one.

It was still light out, but it was the time of day when the ocean settles down and everything gets quiet. The sun was going down behind long strips of clouds, shooting out colors.

Sam was on his knees fussing with the stones, lining them up just so, then messing them up again and starting over.

I talked to him about Broccoli. I wanted to say what I remembered best about her, the way we did with Grandma. As long as I kept talking, my cat wasn't dead and under those stones.

Sam stopped and listened to me, saying yes, and yes. When I finished telling how we rescued her and how furious and wild she was then, he started in.

He told me how Broccoli could read his mind. He always pooh-poohs all that stuff, but he told me that when they were nose to nose and her eyes were up close, this queer feeling went through him.

He said, "I knew that she knew me. All the way through, like nobody else. And I didn't have to say anything."

That was the start. We talked a long time while the colors went out of the sky. We told one another stories about her. I'm sorry, it's just between us and Broccoli what all we said.

Finally, we stopped. It was dark, and we went home.

I have to go to sleep now, because I have the two o'clock shift. Dad said to ask at school Monday if anybody wants a kitten. I'll do it, but I don't think it will help any. Those kids . . . well, I'm too tired to think about it.

Oh, one other thing. At supper Sam put down his fork and said he couldn't eat. I can eat anytime, anywhere, but he said he couldn't swallow. That doesn't mean that Sam feels worse than I do.

Mom told him it was okay, he didn't have to eat. My father said, "Let me ask you, son. Remember when we talked about no love, no hurt? I said you have to pay a price for loving? Remember that?"

Sam got out of his chair and made a face like okay, hurry up, so what.

My father said, "Was it worth it, Sam? Would you rather not have known your cat at all so you wouldn't be feeling this way now? Would you have preferred that?"

My brother practically shouted, "I don't know what you're talking about. Leave me alone!"

He went to his room and banged the door shut.

It makes me so mad that he wouldn't say. He knew what Daddy meant. Sam was trying to be like Mr. Nutt, pushing his true feelings away because he didn't want to hurt so much. When I think of what my time here would have been without Broccoli, when I think of not ever knowing her . . . Maybe for Sam it wasn't worth it, but for me it was. It was, Miss Hasselbauer.

I can't talk about this anymore. *Click.*

Click. Pearl and Patches are here on the bed with me, the only kittens left. The others I gave away, and I'll tell you about that in a minute. Pearl is the blackest, and Patch I already told you about. He's the first one I held. If only I could stick these two babies in my pocket and smuggle them home on the airplane. What could they do to me? Throw me out the airplane window?

I just looked at Sam's calendar. He still crosses out the days, so I know how many are left. Two weeks, three days, and two kittens to go.

We almost lost the kittens because of feeding them regular milk. They were so sick they hardly moved and upchucked and everything. Mom called a vet and found out what to do. They are all okay now. You can't feed baby kittens regular milk is all. Mom was told that if you can't find a mother cat who is nursing and will take them on, you have to get a special milk formula for them. She bought lots of cans of it and some bottles to feed them with. You have to burp them after, just like a regular baby.

I'll tell you how I found homes for the other three.

We were getting desperate. We see signs, "Free kittens," when we drive around, so we know that lots of people want to give them away.

Eddie came up with an idea that sounded pretty good, so a couple of days ago we tried it. Mom drove us to the shopping mall with the babies in their box. Sam carried the box around, and I held up a sign I made. "Your lucky day. Free baby kittens."

No takers. Lots of little kids wanting to hold them and pet them, but no parents saying yes.

There was one other thing I hadn't done yet. Yesterday I went to school with the pictures Sam took of Broccoli and the babies. I was going to have to tell the class something very personal, and I didn't want to in the worst way. I told myself all the way to school that it was for Broccoli and I had to.

We were supposed to give our oral book reports in English class. When I got called on, I asked Mrs. Chun if I could tell the class something important instead.

She asked what it was, and I said it was about my cat. She said, "Sara, didn't you do your assignment?"

I told her that I had read all the books on the reading list, but something came up. "Please, let me!" I said and clasped my hands, praying she would. Mrs. Chun doesn't know how I hate to beg.

Well, maybe she does, because she looked at me hard for a second and told me I could go ahead.

You know how your voice gets shaky and your hands get sweaty when you're nervous? They were all looking at me, and I didn't have any friends out there.

Broccoli's picture helped me. I held it up to show them and said, "This is my cat. I mean, this was my cat."

I said, "When we first came here, I had nobody, and my grandmother was sick." That was the first private thing I ever told anybody in that class, but they had to know why Broccoli was so important.

I told about the rescue and how it had to be a secret and how she got her name. As I got going it was like making one of my tapes for you, Miss Hasselbauer. I think doing that helped me and helped Broccoli. I was able to talk to them the way I do to you.

I told them the whole story right up to the time we found her in the pool. Except I left out Eddie. He's separate.

I showed them pictures of the babies and passed them around. Some kids got up from their seats to crowd around the pictures.

I told them I was going home soon and we had to find a home for Broccoli's kittens. I told them that's why I was telling them all this. I said, please, some-body, take one of my kittens. It will be like Broccoli, and you'll love it.

Lots of kids raised their hands and said they would ask their parents. The class asked me questions and they said things about their own pets and grand-parents, and I felt different with them. It was like Broc-coli was everybody's cat and they knew just how it was for me.

Miss Hasselbauer, you told me that people were pretty much the same at heart. Privately I didn't see how, but yesterday for once I did. I wish I could start the whole term over again. Not everything, but just how I was with them.

I went home singing to myself. I thought, no more problems.

I hear Eddie at the door, talking to my mom. I have to go. *Click.*

Click. I'm so bursting. I'll take this part out, but I have to tell it first.

What do people do when they get what they want most? How do they stand it?

Mom and Eddie were still at the door when I came out of my room. Mom was leaning against it and Eddie was just inside. He was carrying a bundle wrapped up in brown paper.

She was talking to him about how he could come for a visit sometime, he was welcome. She told him that if he was on the mainland this summer, visiting his mother in Arizona, he could take some more time and come to Boston. Stay with us for a while. Would he like her to arrange this with his father?

I heard her say this. Inside my head, I was saying, oh please. I heard Eddie say yes.

He was looking at me, not Mom, when he said yes. Right then I knew it was starting.

He said to me, "Hey, Sara."

I said it back to him.

Mom said, "What are we doing standing here? Come on in, Eddie. Sam's in his room. I have to finish typing something up, so excuse me. Don't forget what I told you. You come see us."

She left us standing there at the door together, and all of a sudden I didn't know what to do with my arms or legs. They had gotten thick or something. It was all because of how he looked at me. It was like that time when I woke him to tell him his father was there and he put his hand on my face. He was looking at me that same way.

Then he looked away from me and said, "How are the kittens?"

I tried to talk natural. I told him about telling my class about Broccoli and how only three kids were allowed to take home a kitten. I told him that just this afternoon the kids came home with me to pick out the one they wanted. Two kittens were left now. They were in a box in my room, and we didn't know what we were going to do with them.

He said, "Only two left? That's good. That makes it easier."

I asked him what he meant. I also wanted to know what was in the bundle.

He wouldn't say. He told me that he'd tell me all about it, only later. He asked me if he could see the kittens. All this time there was this . . . something special between us.

He sat on my bed and picked up Pearl. I watched his hands. He held her up and said, "I'm going to see you this summer," and I wondered how he would. Then I realized it was me he meant, not Pearl.

I sat down next to him on the bed. I wasn't doing much thinking. My brains were asleep and everything else wide awake. I smelled the sun and the dirt on him. My arm prickled where it touched his shirt.

He turned his head, and I felt his breath on my face. Then he kissed me.

He landed on me so quickly I didn't have time to close my eyes or get my mouth ready. All I felt at the most important moment of my whole life was that the fuzz on his lip tickled. It was over before I could really get into it, like I missed the whole thing.

In all the times I dreamed about him kissing me, not once was it a flop. My eyes were always closed and his lips were soft, and we knew just what to do. It wasn't like that at all.

After, we were both kind of embarrassed and could hardly look at each other. Then we went to Sam's room, with Eddie carrying his bundle.

But now, now that I'm alone and I can think about it, everything I missed comes back. It's like that time in the waves at the Memorial Picnic and I got stung by the jellyfish. When I think of Eddie kissing me, the shock of it goes through me like that. And anytime I want, I can remember and feel his lips on my lips and be stung again. *Click.*

Click. Hi, everybody. You know how you get when something wild is about to happen? I can't sit still, I can hardly get these words out. Get ready for Operation SBK. That's the code name for it. It means Save Broccoli's Kids.

The way it started was that this afternoon Eddie came here with a bundle and wouldn't tell me what it was until we got to Sam's room. He put it down on Sam's bed and said to us, "In here is dynamite. You want to save those kittens? My old man told me how, and he didn't even know it. Wait'll you see!"

He opened the package, and all it was was a messy old blanket. It stank, too.

Sam said, "This is it? This old blanket? You kidding?"

He had been busy packing up his rock collection and wasn't so happy to see us in the first place.

Eddie said, "Hey, I told you, man. My own father says this, and he knows what he's talking about. Yesterday, I heard him tell a customer how to get a cat to take on kittens not her own. Like adopt. He says to the lady, 'You get something that has the smell on it, something the cat used with her own kittens. You rub the smell on the new ones, and maybe she'll take them on.'"

He picked up the blanket. "So I brought you the smell. Princess Di's blanket. You put your kittens on this for a couple days, let them mess around on it. Then we see what Princess Di thinks. She's so dumb she'll think they belong to her. You don't want it? No sweat." He started to shove it back in the paper bag.

Sam grabbed the bag away from him. "Hey, wait a minute. Let me get this straight. We rub the kittens with this blanket so maybe it will fool Princess Di. She'll take care of them, let them nurse and all that. Right?"

I said, "That would be so great, Eddie. But how? How do we do that? Will your father let us?"

Eddie thought that was a big joke. "Not in a million years," he said.

That's when we planned Operation SBK.

See, I'm going to put the blanket in Pearl and Patch's box for a couple of days. Let them soak in it. Friday night, that's three days from now, Mr. Nutt goes to his lodge meeting. We sneak the kittens into the window with Princess Di while he's gone, and hope for the best.

Princess isn't the only hitch. It's Mr. Nutt. Not even Eddie could say what will happen when his father sees our blackies with his whities. Eddie says he can't promise that his father will keep the kittens even if Princess Di loves them.

I didn't think anyone could be that cruel. Sam was biting his lip and thinking. Finally, he said not to worry, he would figure out a way that would make Mr. Nutt keep Broccoli's babies. I believe him. My brother is smart when he wants to be.

At supper tonight my parents told us that we would be turning over the kittens to the pound at the end of this week. We are going home next Tuesday, and it has to be done. They said, sorry.

If it weren't for SBK, I would really be in the pits. *Click.*

Click. Dear Miss Hasselbauer and everybody.

Today is Sunday and we're packing up to go home in two days. I'll take this last tape on the airplane with me and won't even pack it in my suitcase, just to keep it safe. I'll bring it in to class maybe next Thursday if I'm still not too dopey from jet lag. It's hard to believe that in four more days I'll be sitting in class with all of you, sitting in my own seat. It's what I dream of.

Our parents were at a good-bye party Friday night, so we didn't have to explain anything in advance. Operation SBK was beginning.

When Eddie phoned us to say the coast was clear, we

wrapped Pearl and Patch in the blanket, Princess Di's blanket, and took them to the shopping center.

It's a pretty spooky place at night with everything closed. Eddie was waiting for us out front of the pet store.

Princess Di was in the window on her side, nursing her kittens.

It was a snap. Eddie had already turned off the burglar alarm. He didn't even want to turn on the lights, just in case. He put the kittens in the window with Princess Di, then we ran outside to watch what would happen.

Eddie had put them close to her. She got up and sniffed them all over and went back to her own babies. She wasn't interested.

I thought, oh no!, it wasn't going to work. But then, she got up again, and, as if they had just wandered off for a moment, she nudged them over to the others and settled herself down again. Pearl and Patch fastened on her like they were both saying, "Wow! At last! The real thing."

Princess Di had accepted them. It was done.

Now the tricky part. We had to keep it done.

That Friday was our last day at school. Sam had it all planned out in advance, just like he said he would. I think he's a genius.

I had made the announcement in class, just the way Sam told me to.

Friday afternoon he had telephoned the newspaper to speak to my mother's reporter friend, Clara Pilapil. I was standing right there, so I could see how much he liked talking to her.

First he asked her if she remembered him. What she said back made him smile at the telephone. He told her what we were going to do that night and why. He asked her would she come to the pet store early tomorrow morning? Yes, he knew it was Saturday, but could she come? He told her, "It would make a terrific human interest story for your column."

By the time Sam hung up, he was thanking her all over the place.

He told me after that she said she would be there only because he asked her to, and that she couldn't promise anything. She had told him to let her know if the SBK plan didn't work out.

Well, I already told you the plan worked fine.

Early yesterday morning, Sam and I were at the pet store before it opened. So was Eddie.

We watched Princess Di with her four babies, two black and two white. It was such a sight. I said to Broccoli in my heart, "Okay, how do you like it so far?" I said the same thing inside me to my grandma because, don't laugh, I pictured her with Broccoli on her lap, both of them watching all this.

Sam was squatting down so he could look the princess in the eye. Maybe he thought he could talk to Princess Di the way he did with Broccoli. Her eyes were half closed, and she looked either very sleepy or very contented with her family. I don't know her well enough to tell.

People were wandering around the mall, waiting for the stores to open. Some of them looked at the window as they passed by, and what they saw stopped them cold. We were gathering a crowd, and the stores hadn't even opened yet.

Pretty soon Doris and Titus from my class came, and then about six more, Anitra and Sharyll and Jason Chang, who I thought hated me, and some others. I had told them when to come and why, but it still seemed a miracle that they actually showed up. I was excited like a hostess, going from one to the other, thanking them and showing them the cat family. "Just wait," I told them. "You'll be in the newspapers."

Sam kept looking at his watch and then up and down the mall. He was all flushed and worried because Miss Pilapil wasn't there yet.

Eddie said, "Uh-oh, here comes Pop. Watch the fireworks."

Sam said in my ear, "We blew it. She's not going to come." He meant the newspaper lady.

Mr. Nutt had to push some people away to get to the store. "Let me through here. Don't block the entrance. Make way. What's going on here?"

He looked at Princess Di in the window feeding her own two kittens plus two more.

Think of a lion roaring. Think of a volcano erupting.

"Eddie!"

"Here, Pa."

Mr. Nutt had his hand on Eddie's shoulder, and just then a camera flashed.

"Hold it!" said Clara Pilapil. She was there! Sam ran over to her.

More flashes went off. She took lots of pictures of Princess Di and her four kittens.

Miss Pilapil was so pretty with her bouncy hair and snappy dark eyes and wonderful smile. Actually, she was laughing all over. "I'm from the *Bulletin*," she said to Mr. Nutt. "Congratulations. I love it! Pure Hawaii, that's what your cat represents. The mix, the melting pot. My readers will get a kick out of this."

I saw her turn and wink at Sam.

It was time for my friends from class to get into the act. Like I told them, they rushed up to Mr. Nutt. They crowded around him, telling him how much they love the kittens and could they come to see them every day. Could they, please? They would bring their parents. They would bring their friends. This was the best pet store on the island.

Clara Pilapil took a picture of them jumping around Eddie's father and pointing to the mixed-up cat family.

Well, what could poor Mr. Nutt do then? You never saw such a seesaw face. It went down when he looked at his precious Princess and her slum kittens. Up when he heard the fuss made over him.

Eddie and I were watching all this from the entrance to the store. Sam came over to be with us, so that made three worried people.

"You know your father best," I said to Eddie. "What's he going to do?" My stomach hurt, I was so nervous. Sam wasn't too cool either. His fists were up to his chest, like he was waiting to be punched.

Eddie didn't take his eyes off Miss Pilapil and his father. They were standing close together, talking a mile a minute. She's tiny compared to him, and when he smiles and means it, he's not so bad. They were not talking about the kittens. Anyone could see that.

What Eddie did was pretend to be a radio announcer telling what was going on between those two like it was a baseball game.

"She steps up to him, ready to bat. Yep, there she

goes. One hand lands on Pop's arm. Will she strike out? No, the poor guy doesn't have a chance. He takes the hand. He holds it for a count of one, two . . . will he go to three? He does! He says something to the lady. It's a question. What could it be, folks? Hold it, hold it! We've got an answer here. The lady says yes."

Eddie stopped announcing and just stared at his father with happy eyes. He said to us, "My pop hasn't gone out on a date for months. I think he has something going here with Miss Hawaii. He won't throw out your kittens. Not after this. We did it! Right, Sam?"

My brother can hide his feelings, but not from me anymore. I knew he was jealous of Mr. Nutt, but he said, "Right!" to Eddie and gave him this handshake. Eddie put my hand on top of theirs, and we all shook hands.

Mr. Nutt and Miss Pilapil were getting along great. No more seesaw face for him. It was only up.

He opened the store. When he was about to step inside, he saw the three of us, me and Sam and Eddie, side by side, standing near the door, watching him. I thought, uh-oh, here it comes, we're all going to get it.

He stopped, looked us over for a second, and nodded his head as if he knew exactly who did what. He shook his head at Eddie, but the corners of his mouth lifted. He winked at Sam and me, and went inside.

Well, so that's it. We're finished here. All done.

Hey, Miss Hasselbauer. Hey, everybody. I'm coming home. *Click.*

ABOUT THE AUTHOR

JAN SLEPIAN was born and grew up in New York City. She majored in psychology at Brooklyn College and did graduate work in clinical psychology at the University of Washington. She is the author of many children's books, among them the widely acclaimed *The Alfred Summer.* Ms. Slepian lives and writes in Summit, New Jersey.

TIMBERWOOD MIDDLE
SCHOOL
READING DEPT.

APPLE PAPERBACKS

Letters
home

Sara had been happy back home in Boston. She fit in—she had friends and knew the ropes at school. Then her family moved to Hawaii for five months.

Her parents think she'll enjoy it, that it will broaden her. She doesn't and it won't. The kids at school aren't nice to her, she doesn't know anyone except her dopey brother, and she misses her friends.

But there are a few good things about being away. One is making the cassette tapes that she sends to her old classmates to keep in touch. And another is Broccoli, the wild cat she and her brother discover. Taking care of Broccoli leads Sara to a new friend, and a whole new look at Hawaii, her brother, and herself.

An ALA Notable Children's Book

★ "Handled with sensitivity and humor..."
　　　　　—<u>School Library Journal</u>, *starred review*

★ "...a rich, robust story..."
　　　　　—<u>Booklist</u>, *starred review*

♦ "Another fine, accessible book from an accomplished author."
　　　　　—<u>Kirkus</u>, *pointed review*

ISBN 0-590-29321-4

EAN

9 780590 293211

90000 >

SCHOLASTIC INC.